Contents

1 Introduction

Why choose Edexcel GCSE in Combined Science?

Supporting success in science

Science matters. That's why we've built the most inclusive GCSE (9–1) courses, so every student can enjoy science and succeed in their studies.

Every student is different. With the same science and equal number of exams across our tiered qualifications, you can structure the courses in the ways that mean you can best support and stretch your students together.

Our specifications are straightforward, and our selection of core practicals are designed to help bring science learning to life. And when it comes to our assessments, they're shaped to encourage all students to best show what they know and can do.

Supporting you in planning and implementing this qualification

Planning

- Our **Getting Started** guide gives you an overview of the new GCSE qualifications to help you to get to grips with the changes to content and assessment and to help you understand what these changes mean for you and your students.
- We will give you editable **schemes of work** that you can adapt to suit your department.
- **Our mapping documents** highlight key differences between the new and 2011 qualifications.

Teaching and learning

There will be lots of free teaching and learning support to help you deliver the new qualifications, including:

- a free series of teacher, student and technician worksheets will help cover each element of planning and delivering every core practical
- a free practical guide to help you prepare for the changes to practical assessment
- a free maths guide for scientists to help you embed mathematics in your science teaching.

Preparing for exams

We will also provide a range of resources to help you prepare your students for the assessments, including:

- additional assessment materials to support formative assessments and mock exams
- marked exemplars of student work with examiner commentaries.

ResultsPlus

ResutsPlus provides the most detailed analysis available of your students' exam performance. It can help you identify the topics and skills where further learning would benefit your students.

Get help and support

Our subject advisor service, led by Stephen Nugus and Julius Edwards will ensure you receive help and guidance from us and that you can share ideas and information with other teachers.

Learn more at qualifications.pearson.com

examWizard

examWizard is a free exam preparation tool containing a bank of Edexcel GCSE Science exam questions, mark schemes and examiners' reports. Existing questions will be reviewed and tagged to our new specifications so they can still be used, and question descriptions will be updated.

Qualification at a glance

Content and assessment overview

The Pearson Edexcel Level 1/Level 2 GCSE (9–1) in Combined Science consists of six externally examined papers. These are available at foundation tier and higher tier.

Students must complete all assessments in the same tier.

Students must complete all assessment in May/June in any single year.

Paper 1: Biology 1 (Paper code: 1SC0/1BF, 1SC0/1BH)
Written examination: 1 hour and 10 minutes ***16.67% of the qualification*** ***60 marks***
Content overview Topic 1 – Key concepts in biology, Topic 2 – Cells and control, Topic 3 – Genetics, Topic 4 – Natural selection and genetic modification, Topic 5 – Health, disease and the development of medicines
Assessment overview A mixture of different question styles, including multiple-choice questions, short answer questions, calculations and extended open-response questions.

Paper 2: Biology 2 (Paper code: 1SC0/2BF, 1SC0/2BH)
Written examination: 1 hour and 10 minutes ***16.67% of the qualification*** ***60 marks***
Content overview Topic 1 – Key concepts in biology, Topic 6 – Plant structures and their functions, Topic 7 – Animal coordination, control and homeostasis, Topic 8 – Exchange and transport in animals, Topic 9 – Ecosystems and material cycles
Assessment overview A mixture of different question styles, including multiple-choice questions, short answer questions, calculations and extended open-response questions.

Paper 3: Chemistry 1 (Paper code: 1SC0/1CF, 1SC0/1CH)
Written examination: 1 hour and 10 minutes ***16.67% of the qualification*** ***60 marks***
Content overview Topic 1 – Key concepts in chemistry, Topic 2 – States of matter and mixtures, Topic 3 – Chemical changes, Topic 4 – Extracting metals and equilibria
Assessment overview A mixture of different question styles, including multiple-choice questions, short answer questions, calculations and extended open-response questions.

Paper 4: Chemistry 2 (*Paper code: 1SC0/2CF, 1SC0/2CH)
Written examination: 1 hour and 10 minutes ***16.67% of the qualification*** ***60 marks***
Content overview Topic 1 – Key concepts in chemistry, Topic 6 – Groups in the periodic table, Topic 7 – Rates of reaction and energy changes, Topic 8 – Fuels and Earth science
Assessment overview A mixture of different question styles, including multiple-choice questions, short-answer questions, calculations and extended open-response questions.

Paper 5: Physics 1 (Paper code: 1SC0/1PF, 1SC0/1PH)
Written examination: 1 hour and 10 minutes ***16.67% of the qualification*** ***60 marks***
Content overview Topic 1 – Key concepts of physics, Topic 2 – Motion and forces, Topic 3 – Conservation of energy, Topic 4 – Waves, Topic 5 – Light and the electromagnetic spectrum, Topic 6 – Radioactivity
Assessment overview A mixture of different question styles, including multiple-choice questions, short answer questions, calculations and extended open-response questions.

Paper 6: Physics 2 (Paper code: 1SC0/2PF, 1SC0/2PH)
Written examination: 1 hour 10 minutes ***16.67% of the qualification*** ***60 marks***
Content overview Topic 1 – Key concepts of physics, Topic 8 – Energy - Forces doing work, Topic 9 – Forces and their effects, Topic 10 – Electricity and circuits, Topic 12 – Magnetism and the motor effect, Topic 13 – Electromagnetic induction, Topic 14 – Particle model, Topic 15 – Forces and matter
Assessment overview A mixture of different question styles, including multiple-choice questions, short answer questions, calculations and extended open-response questions.

*See *Appendix 10: Codes* for a description of this code and all other codes relevant to this qualification.

2 Subject content

Qualification aims and objectives

GCSE study in the sciences provides the foundation for understanding the material world. Scientific understanding is changing our lives and is vital to the world's future prosperity. All students should learn essential aspects of the knowledge, methods, processes and uses of science. They should gain appreciation of how the complex and diverse phenomena of the natural world can be described in terms of a small number of key ideas that relate to the sciences and that are both inter-linked and of universal application. These key ideas include:

- the use of conceptual models and theories to make sense of the observed diversity of natural phenomena
- the assumption that every effect has one or more cause
- that change is driven by differences between different objects and systems when they interact
- that many such interactions occur over a distance and over time without direct contact
- that science progresses through a cycle of hypothesis, practical experimentation, observation, theory development and review
- that quantitative analysis is a central element both of many theories and of scientific methods of inquiry.

These key ideas are relevant in different ways and with different emphases in the three subjects as part of combined science. Examples of their relevance are given for each subject in the separate sections below for Biology, Chemistry and Physics components of combined science.

The GCSE in Combined Science should enable students to:

- develop scientific knowledge and conceptual understanding through the specific disciplines of Biology, Chemistry and Physics
- develop understanding of the nature, processes and methods of science, through different types of scientific enquiries that help them to answer scientific questions about the world around them
- develop and learn to apply observational, practical, modelling, enquiry and problem-solving skills in the laboratory, in the field and in other learning environments
- develop their ability to evaluate claims based on science through critical analysis of the methodology, evidence and conclusions, both qualitatively and quantitatively.

Students should study the sciences in ways that help them to develop curiosity about the natural world, that give them an insight into how science works and that enable them to appreciate its relevance to their everyday lives. The scope and nature of the study should be broad, coherent, practical and satisfying. It should encourage students to be inspired, motivated and challenged by the subject and its achievements.

The key ideas specific to the Combined Science content include:

BIOLOGY

- life processes depend on molecules whose structure is related to their function
- the fundamental units of living organisms are cells, which may be part of highly adapted structures including tissues, organs and organ systems, enabling living processes to be performed effectively

- living organisms may form populations of single species, communities of many species and ecosystems, interacting with each other, with the environment and with humans in many different ways
- living organisms are interdependent and show adaptations to their environment
- life on Earth is dependent on photosynthesis in which green plants and algae trap light from the Sun to fix carbon dioxide and combine it with hydrogen from water to make organic compounds and oxygen
- organic compounds are used as fuels in cellular respiration to allow the other chemical reactions necessary for life
- the chemicals in ecosystems are continually cycling through the natural world
- the characteristics of a living organism are influenced by its genome and its interaction with the environment
- evolution occurs by a process of natural selection and accounts both for biodiversity and how organisms are all related to varying degrees.

CHEMISTRY

- matter is composed of tiny particles called atoms and there are about 100 different naturally occurring types of atoms called elements
- elements show periodic relationships in their chemical and physical properties
- these periodic properties can be explained in terms of the atomic structure of the elements
- atoms bond by either transferring electrons from one atom to another or by sharing electrons
- the shapes of molecules (groups of atoms bonded together) and the way giant structures are arranged is of great importance in terms of the way they behave
- there are barriers to reaction so reactions occur at different rates
- chemical reactions take place in only three different ways:
  - proton transfer
  - electron transfer
  - electron sharing
- energy is conserved in chemical reactions so can therefore be neither created nor destroyed.

PHYSICS

- the use of models, as in the particle model of matter or the wave models of light and of sound
- the concept of cause and effect in explaining such links as those between force and acceleration, or between changes in atomic nuclei and radioactive emissions
- the phenomena of 'action at a distance' and the related concept of the field as the key to analysing electrical, magnetic and gravitational effects
- that differences, for example between pressures or temperatures or electrical potentials, are the drivers of change
- that proportionality, for example between weight and mass of an object or between force and extension in a spring, is an important aspect of many models in science
- that physical laws and models are expressed in mathematical form.

All of these key ideas will be assessed as part of this qualification, through the subject content.

Working scientifically

The GCSE in Combined Science requires students to develop the skills, knowledge and understanding of working scientifically. Working scientifically will be assessed through examination and the completion of the eight core practicals.

1 Development of scientific thinking

- a Understand how scientific methods and theories develop over time.
- b Use a variety of models, such as representational, spatial, descriptive, computational and mathematical, to solve problems, make predictions and to develop scientific explanations and an understanding of familiar and unfamiliar facts.
- c Appreciate the power and limitations of science, and consider any ethical issues that may arise.
- d Explain everyday and technological applications of science; evaluate associated personal, social, economic and environmental implications; and make decisions based on the evaluation of evidence and arguments.
- e Evaluate risks both in practical science and the wider societal context, including perception of risk in relation to data and consequences.
- f Recognise the importance of peer review of results and of communicating results to a range of audiences.

2 Experimental skills and strategies

- a Use scientific theories and explanations to develop hypotheses.
- b Plan experiments or devise procedures to make observations, produce or characterise a substance, test hypotheses, check data or explore phenomena.
- c Apply a knowledge of a range of techniques, instruments, apparatus and materials to select those appropriate to the experiment.
- d Carry out experiments appropriately, having due regard to the correct manipulation of apparatus, the accuracy of measurements and health and safety considerations.
- e Recognise when to apply a knowledge of sampling techniques to ensure any samples collected are representative.
- f Make and record observations and measurements using a range of apparatus and methods.
- g Evaluate methods and suggest possible improvements and further investigations.

3 Analysis and evaluation

Apply the cycle of collecting, presenting and analysing data, including:

- a presenting observations and other data using appropriate methods
- b translating data from one form to another
- c carrying out and representing mathematical and statistical analysis

d representing distributions of results and making estimations of uncertainty

e interpreting observations and other data (presented in verbal, diagrammatic, graphical, symbolic or numerical form), including identifying patterns and trends, making inferences and drawing conclusions

f presenting reasoned explanations including relating data to hypotheses

g being objective, evaluating data in terms of accuracy, precision, repeatability and reproducibility and identifying potential sources of random and systematic error

h communicating the scientific rationale for investigations, methods used, findings and reasoned conclusions through paper-based and electronic reports and presentations using verbal, diagrammatic, graphical, numerical and symbolic forms.

4 Scientific vocabulary, quantities, units, symbols and nomenclature

a Use scientific vocabulary, terminology and definitions.

b Recognise the importance of scientific quantities and understand how they are determined.

c Use SI units (e.g. kg, g, mg; km, m, mm; kJ, J) and IUPAC chemical nomenclature unless inappropriate.

d Use prefixes and powers of ten for orders of magnitude (e.g. tera, giga, mega, kilo, centi, milli, micro and nano).

e Interconvert units.

f Use an appropriate number of significant figures in calculation.

Practical work

The content includes 18 mandatory core practicals, indicated as an entire specification point in italics.

Students must carry out all 18 of the mandatory core practicals listed below.

Biology

Core practicals:

1.6 *Investigate biological specimens using microscopes, including magnification calculations and labelled scientific drawings from observations*

1.10 *Investigate the effect of pH on enzyme activity*

1.16 *Investigate osmosis in potatoes*

6.5 *Investigate the effect of light intensity on the rate of photosynthesis*

8.11 *Investigate the rate of respiration in living organisms*

9.5 *Investigate the relationship between organisms and their environment using field-work techniques, including quadrats and belt transects*

Chemistry

Core practicals:

2.11 *Investigate the composition of inks using simple distillation and paper chromatography*

3.6 *Investigate the change in pH on adding powdered calcium hydroxide/calcium oxide to a fixed volume of dilute hydrochloric acid*

3.17 *Investigate the preparation of pure, dry hydrated copper sulfate crystals starting from copper oxide including the use of a water bath*

3.31 *Investigate the electrolysis of copper sulfate solution with inert electrodes and copper electrodes*

7.1 *Investigate the effects of changing the conditions of a reaction on the rates of chemical reactions by:*

a measuring the production of a gas (in the reaction between hydrochloric acid and marble chips)

b observing a colour change (in the reaction between sodium thiosulfate and hydrochloric acid)

Physics

Core practicals:

2.19 *Investigate the relationship between force, mass and acceleration by varying the masses added to trolleys*

4.17 *Investigate the suitability of equipment to measure the speed, frequency and wavelength of a wave in a solid and a fluid*

5.9 *Investigate refraction in rectangular glass blocks in terms of the interaction of electromagnetic waves with matter*

10.17 *Construct electrical circuits to:*

a investigate the relationship between potential difference, current and resistance for a resistor and a filament lamp

b test series and parallel circuits using resistors and filament lamps

14.3 *Investigate the densities of solid and liquids*

14.11 *Investigate the properties of water by determining the specific heat capacity of water and obtaining a temperature-time graph for melting ice*

15.6 *Investigate the extension and work done when applying forces to a spring*

Students will need to use their knowledge and understanding of these practical techniques and procedures in the written assessments.

Centres must confirm that each student has completed the 18 mandatory core practicals.

Students need to record the work that they have undertaken for the 18 mandatory core practicals. The practical record must include the knowledge, skills and understanding they have derived from the practical activities. Centres must complete and submit a Practical Science Statement (see *Appendix 7*) to confirm that all students have completed the 18 mandatory core practicals. This must be submitted to Pearson by 15th April in the year that the students will sit their examinations. Any failure by centres to provide this Practical Science Statement will be treated as malpractice and/or maladministration.

Scientific diagrams should be included, where appropriate, to show the set-up and to record the apparatus and procedures used in practical work.

It is important to realise that these core practicals are the minimum number of practicals that should be taken during the course. Suggested additional practicals are given beneath the content at the end of each topic. The 18 mandatory core practicals cover all aspects of the apparatus and techniques listed in *Appendix 6: Apparatus and techniques*. This appendix also includes more detailed instructions for each core practical, which must be followed.

Safety is an overriding requirement for all practical work. Centres are responsible for ensuring appropriate safety procedures are followed whenever their students complete practical work.

These core practicals may be reviewed and amended if changes are required to the apparatus and techniques listed by the Department for Education. Pearson may also review and amend the core practicals if necessary. Centres will be told as soon as possible about any changes to core practicals.

Qualification content

The following notation is used in the tables that show the content for this qualification:

- text in **bold** indicates content that is for higher tier only
- entire specification points in italics indicates a core practical.

Mathematics

Maths skills that can be assessed in relation to a specification point are referenced in the maths column, next to this specification point. Please see *Appendix 1: Mathematical skills* for full details of each maths skill.

After each topic of content in this specification, there are details relating to the 'Use of mathematics' which contains the Combined Science specific mathematic skills that are found within each topic of content in the document *Combined Science GCSE subject content*, published by the Department for Education (DfE) in June 2014. The reference in brackets after each statement refers to the mathematical skills from *Appendix 1*.

Equations

The required physics equations are listed in *Appendix 4: Equations in Physics*. The first list shows the equations which students are expected to recall for use in the exam papers. These equations may sometimes be given in the exam papers. The equations required for higher tier only are shown in bold text. These equations are also listed in the specification content, in the physics section.

Biology

Topics common to Paper 1 and Paper 2

Topic 1 – Key concepts in biology

Students should:		Maths skills
1.1	Explain how the sub-cellular structures of eukaryotic and prokaryotic cells are related to their functions, including: a animal cells – nucleus, cell membrane, mitochondria and ribosomes b plant cells – nucleus, cell membrane, cell wall, chloroplasts, mitochondria, vacuole and ribosomes c bacteria – chromosomal DNA, plasmid DNA, cell membrane, ribosomes and flagella	
1.2	Describe how specialised cells are adapted to their function, including: a sperm cells – acrosome, haploid nucleus, mitochondria and tail b egg cells – nutrients in the cytoplasm, haploid nucleus and changes in the cell membrane after fertilisation c ciliated epithelial cells	
1.3	Explain how changes in microscope technology, including electron microscopy, have enabled us to see cell structures with more clarity and detail than in the past and increased our understanding of the role of sub-cellular structures	
1.4	Demonstrate an understanding of number, size and scale, including the use of estimations and explain when they should be used	1d 2h
1.5	Demonstrate an understanding of the relationship between quantitative units in relation to cells, including: a milli (10^{-3}) b micro (10^{-6}) c nano (10^{-9}) d pico (10^{-12}) **e calculations with numbers written in standard form**	1b 2a 2h
1.6	*Core Practical: Investigate biological specimens using microscopes, including magnification calculations and labelled scientific drawings from observations*	1d 2a, 2h 3b
1.7	Explain the mechanism of enzyme action including the active site and enzyme specificity	

Students should:		Maths skills
1.8	Explain how enzymes can be denatured due to changes in the shape of the active site	
1.9	Explain the effects of temperature, substrate concentration and pH on enzyme activity	2c, 2f 4a, 4c
1.10	*Core Practical: Investigate the effect of pH on enzyme activity*	2c, 2f 4a, 4c
1.11	Demonstrate an understanding of rate calculations for enzyme activity	1a, 1c
1.12	Explain the importance of enzymes as biological catalysts in the synthesis of carbohydrates, proteins and lipids and their breakdown into sugars, amino acids and fatty acids and glycerol	
1.15	Explain how substances are transported into and out of cells, including by diffusion, osmosis and active transport	
1.16	*Core Practical: Investigate osmosis in potatoes*	1c 2b, 2f 4a, 4c
1.17	Calculate percentage gain and loss of mass in osmosis	1a, 1c 4a, 4c

Specification points 1.13 and 1.14 are in the GCSE in Biology only.

Use of mathematics

- Demonstrate an understanding of number, size and scale and the quantitative relationship between units (2a and 2h).
- Use estimations and explain when they should be used (1d).
- Carry out rate calculations for chemical reactions (1a and 1c).
- **Calculate with numbers written in standard form (1b).**
- Plot, draw and interpret appropriate graphs (4a, 4b, 4c and 4d).
- Translate information between numerical and graphical forms (4a).
- Construct and interpret frequency tables and diagrams, bar charts and histograms (2c).
- Use a scatter diagram to identify a correlation between two variables (2g).
- Understand and use simple compound measures such as the rate of a reaction (1a and 1c).
- Calculate the percentage gain and loss of mass (1c).
- Calculate arithmetic means (2b).
- Carry out rate calculations (1a and 1c).

Suggested practicals

- Investigate the effect of different concentrations of digestive enzymes, using and evaluating models of the alimentary canal.
- Investigate the effect of temperatures and concentration on enzyme activity.
- Investigate plant and animal cells with a light microscope.
- Investigate the effect of concentration on rate of diffusion.

Topics for Paper 1

Topic 2 – Cells and control

Students should:		Maths skills
2.1	Describe mitosis as part of the cell cycle, including the stages interphase, prophase, metaphase, anaphase and telophase and cytokinesis	
2.2	Describe the importance of mitosis in growth, repair and asexual reproduction	
2.3	Describe the division of a cell by mitosis as the production of two daughter cells, each with identical sets of chromosomes in the nucleus to the parent cell, and that this results in the formation of two genetically identical diploid body cells	
2.4	Describe cancer as the result of changes in cells that lead to uncontrolled cell division	
2.5	Describe growth in organisms, including: a cell division and differentiation in animals b cell division, elongation and differentiation in plants	
2.6	Explain the importance of cell differentiation in the development of specialised cells	
2.7	Demonstrate an understanding of the use of percentiles charts to monitor growth	1c 4a
2.8	Describe the function of embryonic stem cells, stem cells in animals and meristems in plants	1d
2.9	Discuss the potential benefits and risks associated with the use of stem cells in medicine	
2.13	Explain the structure and function of sensory receptors, sensory neurones, relay neurones in the CNS, motor neurones and synapses in the transmission of electrical impulses, including the axon, dendron, myelin sheath and the role of neurotransmitters	2g 4a, 4c
2.14	Explain the structure and function of a reflex arc including sensory, relay and motor neurones	

Specification points 2.10, 2.11, 2.12, 2.15, 2.16 and 2.17 are in the GCSE in Biology only.

Use of mathematics

- Use estimations and explain when they should be used (1d).
- Use percentiles and calculate percentage gain and loss of mass (1c).
- Translate information between numerical and graphical forms (4a).
- Use a scatter diagram to identify a correlation between two variables (2g).
- Extract and interpret information from graphs, charts and tables (2c and 4a).
- Understand and use percentiles (1c).

Suggested practicals

- Investigate human responses to external stimuli.
- Investigate reaction times.
- Investigate the speed of transmission of electrical impulses in the nervous system.

Topic 3 – Genetics

Students should:		Maths skills
3.3	Explain the role of meiotic cell division, including the production of four daughter cells, each with half the number of chromosomes, and that this results in the formation of genetically different haploid gametes The stages of meiosis are not required	
3.4	Describe DNA as a polymer made up of: a two strands coiled to form a double helix b strands linked by a series of complementary base pairs joined together by weak hydrogen bonds	
3.5	Describe the genome as the entire DNA of an organism and a gene as a section of a DNA molecule that codes for a specific protein	
3.6	Explain how DNA can be extracted from fruit	
3.12	Explain why there are differences in the inherited characteristics as a result of alleles	
3.13	Explain the terms: chromosome, gene, allele, dominant, recessive, homozygous, heterozygous, genotype, phenotype, gamete and zygote	
3.14	Explain monohybrid inheritance using genetic diagrams, Punnett squares and family pedigrees	1c 2c, 2e 4a
3.15	Describe how the sex of offspring is determined at fertilisation, using genetic diagrams	1c 2c, 2e 4a
3.16	Calculate and analyse outcomes (using probabilities, ratios and percentages) from monohybrid crosses and pedigree analysis for dominant and recessive traits	1c 2c, 2e 4a
3.19	State that most phenotypic features are the result of multiple genes rather than single gene inheritance	
3.20	Describe the causes of variation that influence phenotype, including: a genetic variation – different characteristics as a result of mutation and sexual reproduction b environmental variation – different characteristics caused by an organism's environment (acquired characteristics)	
3.21	Discuss the outcomes of the Human Genome Project and its potential applications within medicine	

Students should:	Maths skills
3.22 State that there is usually extensive genetic variation within a population of a species and that these arise through mutations	
3.23 State that most genetic mutations have no effect on the phenotype, some mutations have a small effect on the phenotype and, rarely, a single mutation will significantly affect the phenotype	

Specification points 3.1, 3.2, 3.7, 3.8, 3.9, 3.10, 3.11, 3.17 and 3.18 are in the GCSE in Biology only.

Use of mathematics

- Use estimations and explain when they should be used (1d).
- Translate information between numerical and graphical forms (4a).
- Extract and interpret information from graphs, charts and tables (2c and 4a).
- Understand and use direct proportions and simple ratios in genetic crosses (1c).
- Understand and use the concept of probability in predicting the outcome of genetic crosses (2e).
- Calculate arithmetic means (2b).

Suggested practicals

- Investigate the variations in a species to illustrate continuous variation and discontinuous variation.
- Investigate inheritance using suitable organisms or models.

Topic 4 – Natural selection and genetic modification

Students should:		Maths skills
4.2	Explain Darwin's theory of evolution by natural selection	
4.3	Explain how the emergence of resistant organisms supports Darwin's theory of evolution including antibiotic resistance in bacteria	2c 4a
4.4	Describe the evidence for human evolution, based on fossils, including: a Ardi from 4.4 million years ago b Lucy from 3.2 million years ago c Leakey's discovery of fossils from 1.6 million years ago	1a, 1b, 1c 4a
4.5	Describe the evidence for human evolution based on stone tools, including: a the development of stone tools over time b how these can be dated from their environment	
4.7	Describe how genetic analysis has led to the suggestion of the three domains rather than the five kingdoms classification method	
4.8	Explain selective breeding and its impact on food plants and domesticated animals	
4.10	Describe genetic engineering as a process which involves modifying the genome of an organism to introduce desirable characteristics	
4.11	**Describe the main stages of genetic engineering including the use of:** **a restriction enzymes** **b ligase** **c sticky ends** **d vectors**	
4.14	Evaluate the benefits and risks of genetic engineering and selective breeding in modern agriculture and medicine, including practical and ethical implications	2c 4a, 4c

Specification points 4.1, 4.6, 4.9, 4.12 and 4.13 are in the GCSE in Biology only.

Use of mathematics

- Translate information between numerical and graphical forms (4a).
- Construct and interpret frequency tables and diagrams, bar charts and histograms (2c).
- Plot and draw appropriate graphs, selecting appropriate scales for axes (4a and 4c).
- Extract and interpret information from graphs, charts and tables (2c and 4a).
- Understand and use direct proportions and simple ratios in genetic crosses (1c).
- Understand and use the concept of probability in predicting the outcome of genetic crosses (2e).

Topic 5 – Health, disease and the development of medicines

Students should:		Maths skills
5.1	Describe health as a state of complete physical, mental and social well-being and not merely the absence of disease or infirmity, as defined by the World Health Organization (WHO)	
5.2	Describe the difference between communicable and non-communicable diseases	
5.3	Explain why the presence of one disease can lead to a higher susceptibility to other diseases	2c, 2d, 2g 4a, 4c
5.4	Describe a pathogen as a disease-causing organism, including viruses, bacteria, fungi and protists	
5.5	Describe some common infections, including: a cholera (bacteria) causes diarrhoea b tuberculosis (bacteria) causes lung damage c Chalara ash dieback (fungi) causes leaf loss and bark lesions d malaria (protists) causes damage to blood and liver e HIV (virus) destroys white blood cells, leading to the onset of AIDS	
5.6	Explain how pathogens are spread and how this spread can be reduced or prevented, including: a cholera (bacteria) – water b tuberculosis (bacteria) – airborne c Chalara ash dieback (fungi) – airborne d malaria (protists) – animal vectors	
5.8	Explain how sexually transmitted infections (STIs) are spread and how this spread can be reduced or prevented, including: a *Chlamydia* (bacteria) b HIV (virus)	
5.12	Describe how the physical barriers and chemical defences of the human body provide protection from pathogens, including: a physical barriers, including mucus, cilia and skin b chemical defence, including lysozymes and hydrochloric acid	5c

Students should:		Maths skills
5.13	Explain the role of the specific immune system of the human body in defence against disease, including: a exposure to pathogen b the antigens trigger an immune response which causes the production of antibodies c the antigens also trigger production of memory lymphocytes d the role of memory lymphocytes in the secondary response to the antigen	
5.14	Explain the body's response to immunisation using an inactive form of a pathogen	2c, 2g 4a, 4c
5.16	Explain that antibiotics can only be used to treat bacterial infections because they inhibit cell processes in the bacterium but not the host organism.	
5.20	Describe that the process of developing new medicines, including antibiotics, has many stages, including discovery, development, preclinical and clinical testing.	5c
5.23	Describe that many non-communicable human diseases are caused by the interaction of a number of factors, including cardiovascular diseases, many forms of cancer, some lung and liver diseases and diseases influenced by nutrition	
5.24	Explain the effect of lifestyle factors on non-communicable diseases at local, national and global levels, including: a exercise and diet on obesity and malnutrition, including BMI and waist : hip calculations, using the BMI equation: $\text{BMI} = \dfrac{\text{weight (kg)}}{(\text{height (m)})^2}$ b alcohol on liver diseases c smoking on cardiovascular diseases	1a, 1c 2c, 2d, 2g 3b 4a, 4c
5.25	Evaluate some different treatments for cardiovascular disease, including: a life-long medication b surgical procedures c lifestyle changes	1c, 1d 2c 4a, 4c

Specification points 5.7, 5.9, 5.10, 5.11, 5.15, 5.17, 5.18, 5.19, 5.21 and 5.22 are in the GCSE in Biology only.

Use of mathematics

- Plot, draw and interpret appropriate graphs (4a, 4b, 4c and 4d).
- Construct and interpret frequency tables and diagrams, bar charts and histograms (2c).
- Understand the principles of sampling as applied to scientific data (2d).
- Use a scatter diagram to identify a correlation between two variables (2g).
- Calculate cross-sectional areas of bacterial cultures and clear agar jelly using πr^2 (5c).

Suggested practicals

- Investigate antimicrobial properties of plants.
- Investigate the conditions affecting growth of microorganisms (using resazurin dye).

Topics for Paper 2

Topic 6 – Plant structures and their functions

Students should:		Maths skills
6.1	Describe photosynthetic organisms as the main producers of food and therefore biomass	
6.2	Describe photosynthesis in plants and algae as an endothermic reaction that uses light energy to react carbon dioxide and water to produce glucose and oxygen	
6.3	Explain the effect of temperature, light intensity and carbon dioxide concentration as limiting factors on the rate of photosynthesis	2c, 2d, 2g 4a, 4c
6.4	**Explain the interactions of temperature, light intensity and carbon dioxide concentration in limiting the rate of photosynthesis**	4b, 4c, 4d
6.5	*Core Practical: Investigate the effect of light intensity on the rate of photosynthesis*	2c, 2f, 2g 4a, 4c
6.6	**Explain how the rate of photosynthesis is directly proportional to light intensity and inversely proportional to the distance from a light source, including the use of the inverse square law calculation**	2g 3a, 3b 4a, 4b, 4c, 4d
6.7	Explain how the structure of the root hair cells is adapted to absorb water and mineral ions	
6.8	Explain how the structures of the xylem and phloem are adapted to their function in the plant, including: a lignified dead cells in xylem transporting water and minerals through the plant b living cells in phloem using energy to transport sucrose around the plant	
6.9	Describe how water and mineral ions are transported through the plant by transpiration, including the structure and function of the stomata	
6.10	Describe how sucrose is transported around the plant by translocation	
6.12	Explain the effect of environmental factors on the rate of water uptake by a plant, to include light intensity, air movement and temperature	1a, 1c 2b, 2c 4a, 4b, 4c, 4d
6.13	Demonstrate an understanding of rate calculations for transpiration	1a, 1c 2b, 2c 4a, 4b, 4c, 4d

Specification points 6.11, 6.14, 6.15 and 6.16 are in the GCSE in Biology only.

Use of mathematics

- Carry out rate calculations for chemical reactions (1a and 1c).
- Use simple compound measures such as rate (1a, 1c)
- Plot, draw and interpret appropriate graphs (4a, 4b, 4c and 4d).
- Construct and interpret frequency tables and diagrams, bar charts and histograms (2c).
- Understand the principles of sampling as applied to scientific data (2d).
- Use a scatter diagram to identify a correlation between two variables (2g).
- Understand and use simple compound measures such as the rate of a reaction (1a and 1c).
- **Understand and use inverse proportion – the inverse square law and light intensity in the context of factors affecting photosynthesis.**
- Use percentiles and calculate percentage gain and loss of mass (1c).
- Calculate arithmetic means (2b).
- Carry out rate calculations (1a and 1c).

Suggested practicals

- Investigate the effect of pollutants on plant germination and plant growth.
- Investigate tropic responses.
- Investigate the effect of CO_2 concentration or temperature on the rate of photosynthesis.
- Investigate how the structure of the leaf is adapted for photosynthesis.
- Investigate how the loss of water vapour from leaves drives transpiration.
- Investigate the importance of photoperiodicity in plants.

Topic 7 – Animal coordination, control and homeostasis

Students should:		Maths skills
7.1	Describe where hormones are produced and how they are transported from endocrine glands to their target organs, including the pituitary gland, thyroid gland, pancreas, adrenal glands, ovaries and testes	
7.2	**Explain that adrenalin is produced by the adrenal glands to prepare the body for fight or flight, including:** **a increased heart rate** **b increased blood pressure** **c increased blood flow to the muscles** **d raised blood sugar levels by stimulating the liver to change glycogen into glucose**	2c 4a, 4c
7.3	**Explain how thyroxine controls metabolic rate as an example of negative feedback, including:** **a low levels of thyroxine stimulates production of TRH in hypothalamus** **b this causes release of TSH from the pituitary gland** **c TSH acts on the thyroid to produce thyroxine** **d when thyroxine levels are normal thyroxine inhibits the release of TRH and the production of TSH**	2c 4a, 4c
7.4	Describe the stages of the menstrual cycle, including the roles of the hormones oestrogen and progesterone, in the control of the menstrual cycle	4a
7.5	**Explain the interactions of oestrogen, progesterone, FSH and LH in the control of the menstrual cycle, including the repair and maintenance of the uterus wall, ovulation and menstruation**	4a, 4c
7.6	Explain how hormonal contraception influences the menstrual cycle and prevents pregnancy	
7.7	Evaluate hormonal and barrier methods of contraception	2c, 2d 4a
7.8	**Explain the use of hormones in Assisted Reproductive Technology (ART) including IVF and clomifene therapy**	
7.9	Explain the importance of maintaining a constant internal environment in response to internal and external change	
7.13	Explain how the hormone insulin controls blood glucose concentration	
7.14	**Explain how blood glucose concentration is regulated by glucagon**	
7.15	Explain the cause of type 1 diabetes and how it is controlled	
7.16	Explain the cause of type 2 diabetes and how it is controlled	

Students should:	Maths skills
7.17 Evaluate the correlation between body mass and type 2 diabetes including waist:hip calculations and BMI, using the BMI equation: $\text{BMI} = \frac{\text{weight (kg)}}{(\text{height (m)})^2}$	1a, 1c 2c, 2e 3a

Specification points 7.10, 7.11, 7.12, 7.18, 7.19, 7.20, 7.21 and 7.22 are in the GCSE in Biology only.

Uses of mathematics

- Use simple compound measures such as rate (1a, 1c).
- Plot, draw and interpret appropriate graphs (4a, 4b, 4c and 4d).
- Translate information between numerical and graphical forms (4a).
- Construct and interpret frequency tables and diagrams, bar charts and histograms (2c).
- Understand and use percentiles (1c).
- Extract and interpret data from graphs, charts and tables (1c).

Suggested practical

- Investigate the presence of sugar in simulated urine/body fluids.

Topic 8 – Exchange and transport in animals

Students should:		Maths skills
8.1	Describe the need to transport substances into and out of a range of organisms, including oxygen, carbon dioxide, water, dissolved food molecules, mineral ions and urea	
8.2	Explain the need for exchange surfaces and a transport system in multicellular organisms including the calculation of surface area : volume ratio	1a, 1c 5c
8.3	Explain how alveoli are adapted for gas exchange by diffusion between air in the lungs and blood in capillaries	
8.6	Explain how the structure of the blood is related to its function: a red blood cells (erythrocytes) b white blood cells (phagocytes and lymphocytes) c plasma d platelets	1b 2h
8.7	Explain how the structure of the blood vessels is related to their function	1a
8.8	Explain how the structure of the heart and circulatory system is related to its function, including the role of the major blood vessels, the valves and the relative thickness of chamber walls	
8.9	Describe cellular respiration as an exothermic reaction which occurs continuously in living cells to release energy for metabolic processes, including aerobic and anaerobic respiration	
8.10	Compare the process of aerobic respiration with the process of anaerobic respiration	
8.11	*Core Practical: Investigate the rate of respiration in living organisms*	1a 2a, 2c, 2f 4a, 4c
8.12	Calculate heart rate, stroke volume and cardiac output, using the equation cardiac output = stroke volume × heart rate	1a 2a, 2c 3a, 3b 4a, 4c

Specification points 8.4 and 8.5 are in the GCSE in Biology only.

Use of mathematics

- Demonstrate an understanding of number, size and scale and the quantitative relationship between units (2a and 2h).
- **Calculate with numbers written in standard form (1b).**
- Calculate surface area : volume ratios (1c).
- Plot, draw and interpret appropriate graphs (4a, 4b, 4c and 4d).
- Translate information between numerical and graphical forms (4a).
- Construct and interpret frequency tables and diagrams, bar charts and histograms (2c).
- Extract and interpret information from graphs, charts and tables (2c and 4a).
- Use percentiles and calculate percentage gain and loss of mass (1c).

Suggested practicals

- Investigate the effect of glucose concentration on the rate of anaerobic respiration in yeast.
- Investigate the short-term effects of exercise on breathing rate and heart rate.

Topic 9 – Ecosystems and material cycles

Students should:		Maths skills
9.1	Describe the different levels of organisation from individual organisms, populations, communities, to the whole ecosystem	
9.2	Explain how communities can be affected by abiotic and biotic factors, including: a temperature, light, water, pollutants b competition, predation	4a, 4c
9.3	Describe the importance of interdependence in a community	
9.4	Describe how the survival of some organisms is dependent on other species, including parasitism and mutualism	
9.5	*Core Practical: Investigate the relationship between organisms and their environment using field-work techniques, including quadrats and belt transects*	1c, 1d 2b, 2c, 2d, 2f, 2g 4a, 4c
9.6	Explain how to determine the number of organisms in a given area using raw data from field-work techniques, including quadrats and belt transects	1c, 1d 2b, 2c, 2d, 2g 4a, 4c
9.9	Explain the positive and negative human interactions within ecosystems and their impacts on biodiversity, including: a fish farming b introduction of non-indigenous species c eutrophication	2c, 2g 4a, 4c
9.10	Explain the benefits of maintaining local and global biodiversity, including the conservation of animal species and the impact of reforestation	
9.12	Describe how different materials cycle through the abiotic and biotic components of an ecosystem	
9.13	Explain the importance of the carbon cycle, including the processes involved and the role of microorganisms as decomposers	
9.14	Explain the importance of the water cycle, including the processes involved and the production of potable water in areas of drought including desalination	
9.15	Explain how nitrates are made available for plant uptake, including the use of fertilisers, crop rotation and the role of bacteria in the nitrogen cycle	

Specification points 9.7, 9.8, 9.11, 9.16, 9.17, 9.18 and 9.19 are in the GCSE in Biology only.

Use of mathematics

- Calculate surface area : volume ratios (1c).
- Plot, draw and interpret appropriate graphs (4a, 4b, 4c and 4d).
- Understand and use percentiles and calculate percentage gain and loss of mass (1c).
- Translate information between numerical and graphical forms (4a).
- Construct and interpret frequency tables and diagrams, bar charts and histograms (2c).
- Understand the principles of sampling as applied to scientific data (2d).
- Use a scatter diagram to identify a correlation between two variables (2g).
- Calculate the percentage of mass (1c).
- Calculate arithmetic means (2b).
- Extract and interpret information from charts, graphs and tables (2c, 4a).

Suggested practicals

- Investigate tropic responses.
- Investigate animal behaviour using choice chambers.

Chemistry

Topics common to Paper 3 and Paper 4

Formulae, equations and hazards

Students should:		Maths skills
0.1	Recall the formulae of elements, simple compounds and ions	
0.2	Write word equations	
0.3	Write balanced chemical equations, including the use of the state symbols (s), (l), (g) and (aq)	1c
0.4	**Write balanced ionic equations**	1c
0.5	Describe the use of hazard symbols on containers: a to indicate the dangers associated with the contents b to inform people about safe-working precautions with these substances in the laboratory	
0.6	Evaluate the risks in a practical procedure and suggest suitable precautions for a range of practicals including those mentioned in the specification	

Use of mathematics

- Arithmetic computation, ratio when balancing equations (1a and 1c).

Topic 1 – Key concepts in chemistry

Atomic structure

Students should:		Maths skills
1.1	Describe how the Dalton model of an atom has changed over time because of the discovery of subatomic particles	
1.2	Describe the structure of an atom as a nucleus containing protons and neutrons, surrounded by electrons in shells	
1.3	Recall the relative charge and relative mass of: a a proton b a neutron c an electron	
1.4	Explain why atoms contain equal numbers of protons and electrons	
1.5	Describe the nucleus of an atom as very small compared to the overall size of the atom	1d
1.6	Recall that most of the mass of an atom is concentrated in the nucleus	
1.7	Recall the meaning of the term mass number of an atom	
1.8	Describe atoms of a given element as having the same number of protons in the nucleus and that this number is unique to that element	
1.9	Describe isotopes as different atoms of the same element containing the same number of protons but different numbers of neutrons in their nuclei	
1.10	Calculate the numbers of protons, neutrons and electrons in atoms given the atomic number and mass number	3b
1.11	Explain how the existence of isotopes results in relative atomic masses of some elements not being whole numbers	1a, 1c
1.12	**Calculate the relative atomic mass of an element from the relative masses and abundances of its isotopes**	1a, 1c 3a, 3c

Use of mathematics

- Relate size and scale of atoms to objects in the physical world (1d).
- Estimate size and scale of atoms (1d).

The periodic table

Students should:		Maths skills
1.13	Describe how Mendeleev arranged the elements, known at that time, in a periodic table by using properties of these elements and their compounds	
1.14	Describe how Mendeleev used his table to predict the existence and properties of some elements not then discovered	
1.15	Explain that Mendeleev thought he had arranged elements in order of increasing relative atomic mass but this was not always true because of the relative abundance of isotopes of some pairs of elements in the periodic table	
1.16	Explain the meaning of atomic number of an element in terms of position in the periodic table and number of protons in the nucleus	
1.17	Describe that in the periodic table a elements are arranged in order of increasing atomic number, in rows called periods b elements with similar properties are placed in the same vertical columns called groups	
1.18	Identify elements as metals or non-metals according to their position in the periodic table, explaining this division in terms of the atomic structures of the elements	
1.19	Predict the electronic configurations of the first 20 elements in the periodic table as diagrams and in the form, for example 2.8.1	4a 5b
1.20	Explain how the electronic configuration of an element is related to its position in the periodic table	4a

Ionic bonding

Students should:		Maths skills
1.21	Explain how ionic bonds are formed by the transfer of electrons between atoms to produce cations and anions, including the use of dot and cross diagrams	5b
1.22	Recall that an ion is an atom or group of atoms with a positive or negative charge	
1.23	Calculate the numbers of protons, neutrons and electrons in simple ions given the atomic number and mass number	3b
1.24	Explain the formation of ions in ionic compounds from their atoms, limited to compounds of elements in groups 1, 2, 6 and 7	1c 5b
1.25	Explain the use of the endings –ide and –ate in the names of compounds	

Students should:		Maths skills
1.26	Deduce the formulae of ionic compounds (including oxides, hydroxides, halides, nitrates, carbonates and sulfates) given the formulae of the constituent ions	1c
1.27	Explain the structure of an ionic compound as a lattice structure a consisting of a regular arrangement of ions b held together by strong electrostatic forces (ionic bonds) between oppositely-charged ions	5b

Use of mathematics

- Represent three dimensional shapes in two dimensions and vice versa when looking at chemical structures (5b).

Covalent bonding

Students should:		Maths skills
1.28	Explain how a covalent bond is formed when a pair of electrons is shared between two atoms	
1.29	Recall that covalent bonding results in the formation of molecules	
1.30	Recall the typical size (order of magnitude) of atoms and small molecules	1d

Use of mathematics

- Relate size and scale of atoms to objects in the physical world (1d).
- Estimate size and scale of atoms (1d).

Types of substance

Students should:		Maths skills
1.31	Explain the formation of simple molecular, covalent substances, using dot and cross diagrams, including: a hydrogen b hydrogen chloride c water d methane e oxygen f carbon dioxide	5b

Students should:	Maths skills
1.32 Explain why elements and compounds can be classified as: a ionic b simple molecular (covalent) c giant covalent d metallic and how the structure and bonding of these types of substances results in different physical properties, including relative melting point and boiling point, relative solubility in water and ability to conduct electricity (as solids and in solution)	
1.33 Explain the properties of ionic compounds limited to: a high melting points and boiling points, in terms of forces between ions b whether or not they conduct electricity as solids, when molten and in aqueous solution	4a
1.34 Explain the properties of typical covalent, simple molecular compounds limited to: a low melting points and boiling points, in terms of forces between molecules (intermolecular forces) b poor conduction of electricity	4a
1.35 Recall that graphite and diamond are different forms of carbon and that they are examples of giant covalent substances	
1.36 Describe the structures of graphite and diamond	5b
1.37 Explain, in terms of structure and bonding, why graphite is used to make electrodes and as a lubricant, whereas diamond is used in cutting tools	5b
1.38 Explain the properties of fullerenes including C_{60} and graphene in terms of their structures and bonding	5b
1.39 Describe, using poly(ethene) as the example, that simple polymers consist of large molecules containing chains of carbon atoms	5b
1.40 Explain the properties of metals, including malleability and the ability to conduct electricity	5b

Use of mathematics

- Represent three dimensional shapes in two dimensions and vice versa when looking at chemical structures, e.g. allotropes of carbon (5b).
- Translate information between diagrammatic and numerical forms (4a).

Calculations involving masses

Students should:		Maths skills
1.41	Describe the limitations of particular representations and models to, include dot and cross, ball and stick models and two- and three-dimensional representations	5b
1.42	Describe most metals as shiny solids which have high melting points, high density and are good conductors of electricity whereas most non-metals have low boiling points and are poor conductors of electricity	
1.43	Calculate relative formula mass given relative atomic masses	1a, 1c
1.44	Calculate the formulae of simple compounds from reacting masses and understand that these are empirical formulae	1a, 1c 2a
1.45	Deduce: a the empirical formula of a compound from the formula of its molecule b the molecular formula of a compound from its empirical formula and its relative molecular mass	1c
1.46	Describe an experiment to determine the empirical formula of a simple compound such as magnesium oxide	1a, 1c 2a
1.47	Explain the law of conservation of mass applied to: a a closed system including a precipitation reaction in a closed flask b a non-enclosed system including a reaction in an open flask that takes in or gives out a gas	1a
1.48	Calculate masses of reactants and products from balanced equations, given the mass of one substance	1a, 1c 2a
1.49	Calculate the concentration of solutions in g dm^{-3}	1a, 1c 2a 3b, 3c
1.50	**Recall that one mole of particles of a substance is defined as:** **a the Avogadro constant number of particles (6.02×10^{23} atoms, molecules, formulae or ions) of that substance** **b a mass of 'relative particle mass' g**	1b
1.51	**Calculate the number of:** **a moles of particles of a substance in a given mass of that substance and vice versa** **b particles of a substance in a given number of moles of that substance and vice versa** **c particles of a substance in a given mass of that substance and vice versa**	1a, 1b, 1c 3a, 3b, 3c

Students should:	Maths skills
1.52 **Explain why, in a reaction, the mass of product formed is controlled by the mass of the reactant which is not in excess**	1c
1.53 **Deduce the stoichiometry of a reaction from the masses of the reactants and products**	1a, 1c

Use of mathematics

- Arithmetic computation and ratio when determining empirical formulae, balancing equations (1a and 1c).
- Arithmetic computation, ratio, percentage and multistep calculations permeates quantitative chemistry (1a, 1c and 1d).
- **Calculations with numbers written in standard form when using the Avogadro constant (1b).**
- Change the subject of a mathematical equation (3b and 3c).
- Provide answers to an appropriate number of significant figures (2a).
- **Convert units where appropriate particularly from mass to moles (1c).**

Suggested practicals

- Investigate the size of an oil molecule.
- Investigate the properties of a metal, such as electrical conductivity.
- Investigate the different types of bonding: metallic, covalent and ionic.
- Investigate the typical properties of simple and giant covalent compounds and ionic compounds.
- Classify different types of elements and compounds by investigating their melting points and boiling points, solubility in water and electrical conductivity (as solids and in solution), including sodium chloride, magnesium sulfate, hexane, liquid paraffin, silicon(IV) oxide, copper sulfate, and sucrose (sugar).
- Determine the empirical formula of a simple compound.
- Investigate mass changes before and after reactions.
- Determine the formula of a hydrated salt such as copper sulfate by heating to drive off water of crystallisation.

Topics for Paper 3

Topic 2 – States of matter and mixtures

States of matter

Students should:		Maths skills
2.1	Describe the arrangement, movement and the relative energy of particles in each of the three states of matter: solid, liquid and gas	5b
2.2	Recall the names used for the interconversions between the three states of matter, recognising that these are physical changes: contrasted with chemical reactions that result in chemical changes	
2.3	Explain the changes in arrangement, movement and energy of particles during these interconversions	5b
2.4	Predict the physical state of a substance under specified conditions, given suitable data	1d 4a

Use of mathematics

- Translate information between diagrammatic and numerical forms (4a).

Methods of separating and purifying substances

Students should:		Maths skills
2.5	Explain the difference between the use of 'pure' in chemistry compared with its everyday use and the differences in chemistry between a pure substance and a mixture	
2.6	Interpret melting point data to distinguish between pure substances which have a sharp melting point and mixtures which melt over a range of temperatures	1a
2.7	Explain the experimental techniques for separation of mixtures by: a simple distillation b fractional distillation c filtration d crystallisation e paper chromatography	
2.8	Describe an appropriate experimental technique to separate a mixture, knowing the properties of the components of the mixture	

Students should:		Maths skills
2.9	Describe paper chromatography as the separation of mixtures of soluble substances by running a solvent (mobile phase) through the mixture on the paper (the paper contains the stationary phase), which causes the substances to move at different rates over the paper	
2.10	Interpret a paper chromatogram: a to distinguish between pure and impure substances b to identify substances by comparison with known substances c to identify substances by calculation and use of R_f values	3a, 3c 4a
2.11	*Core Practical: Investigate the composition of inks using simple distillation and paper chromatography*	
2.12	Describe how: a waste and ground water can be made potable, including the need for sedimentation, filtration and chlorination b sea water can be made potable by using distillation c water used in analysis must not contain any dissolved salts	

Use of mathematics

- Interpret charts (4a).

Topic 3 – Chemical change

Acids

Students should:		Maths skills
3.1	Recall that acids in solution are sources of hydrogen ions and alkalis in solution are sources of hydroxide ions	
3.2	Recall that a neutral solution has a pH of 7 and that acidic solutions have lower pH values and alkaline solutions higher pH values	
3.3	Recall the effect of acids and alkalis on indicators, including litmus, methyl orange and phenolphthalein	
3.4	**Recall that the higher the concentration of hydrogen ions in an acidic solution, the lower the pH; and the higher the concentration of hydroxide ions in an alkaline solution, the higher the pH**	1c
3.5	**Recall that as hydrogen ion concentration in a solution increases by a factor of 10, the pH of the solution decreases by 1**	1c
3.6	*Core Practical: Investigate the change in pH on adding powdered calcium hydroxide or calcium oxide to a fixed volume of dilute hydrochloric acid*	4a, 4c
3.7	**Explain the terms dilute and concentrated, with respect to amount of substances in solution**	
3.8	**Explain the terms weak and strong acids, with respect to the degree of dissociation into ions**	
3.9	Recall that a base is any substance that reacts with an acid to form a salt and water only	
3.10	Recall that alkalis are soluble bases	
3.11	Explain the general reactions of aqueous solutions of acids with: a metals b metal oxides c metal hydroxides d metal carbonates to produce salts	
3.12	Describe the chemical test for: a hydrogen b carbon dioxide (using limewater)	
3.13	Describe a neutralisation reaction as a reaction between an acid and a base	
3.14	Explain an acid-alkali neutralisation as a reaction in which hydrogen ions (H+) from the acid react with hydroxide ions (OH–) from the alkali to form water	

Students should:		Maths skills
3.15	Explain why, if soluble salts are prepared from an acid and an insoluble reactant: a excess of the reactant is added b the excess reactant is removed c the solution remaining is only salt and water	
3.16	Explain why, if soluble salts are prepared from an acid and a soluble reactant: a titration must be used b the acid and the soluble reactant are then mixed in the correct proportions c the solution remaining, after reaction, is only salt and water	
3.17	*Core Practical: Investigate the preparation of pure, dry hydrated copper sulfate crystals starting from copper oxide including the use of a water bath*	
3.18	Describe how to carry out an acid-alkali titration, using burette, pipette and a suitable indicator, to prepare a pure, dry salt	
3.19	Recall the general rules which describe the solubility of common types of substances in water: a all common sodium, potassium and ammonium salts are soluble b all nitrates are soluble c common chlorides are soluble except those of silver and lead d common sulfates are soluble except those of lead, barium and calcium e common carbonates and hydroxides are insoluble except those of sodium, potassium and ammonium	
3.20	Predict, using solubility rules, whether or not a precipitate will be formed when named solutions are mixed together, naming the precipitate if any	
3.21	Describe the method used to prepare a pure, dry sample of an insoluble salt	

Suggested practicals

- Carry out simple neutralisation reactions of acids, using metal oxides, hydroxides and carbonates.
- Carry out tests for hydrogen and carbon dioxide.
- Prepare an insoluble salt by precipitation.

Electrolytic processes

Students should:		Maths skills
3.22	Recall that electrolytes are ionic compounds in the molten state or dissolved in water	
3.23	Describe electrolysis as a process in which electrical energy, from a direct current supply, decomposes electrolytes	
3.24	Explain the movement of ions during electrolysis, in which: a positively charged cations migrate to the negatively charged cathode b negatively charged anions migrate to the positively charged anode	
3.25	Explain the formation of the products in the electrolysis, using inert electrodes, of some electrolytes, including: a copper chloride solution b sodium chloride solution c sodium sulfate solution d water acidified with sulfuric acid e molten lead bromide (demonstration)	
3.26	Predict the products of electrolysis of other binary, ionic compounds in the molten state	
3.27	**Write half equations for reactions occurring at the anode and cathode in electrolysis**	1c
3.28	**Explain oxidation and reduction in terms of loss or gain of electrons**	
3.29	**Recall that reduction occurs at the cathode and that oxidation occurs at the anode in electrolysis reactions**	
3.30	Explain the formation of the products in the electrolysis of copper sulfate solution, using copper electrodes, and how this electrolysis can be used to purify copper	
3.31	*Core Practical: Investigate the electrolysis of copper sulfate solution with inert electrodes and copper electrodes*	1a 4a, 4b, 4c, 4d

Suggested practicals

- Investigate the electrolysis of:
  - a copper chloride solution
  - b sodium chloride solution
  - c sodium sulfate solution
  - d water acidified with sulfuric acid
  - e molten lead bromide (demonstration).

Topic 4 – Extracting metals and equilibria

Obtaining and using metals

Students should:		Maths skills
4.1	Deduce the relative reactivity of some metals, by their reactions with water, acids and salt solutions	
4.2	**Explain displacement reactions as redox reactions, in terms of gain or loss of electrons**	
4.3	Explain the reactivity series of metals (potassium, sodium, calcium, magnesium, aluminium, (carbon), zinc, iron, (hydrogen), copper, silver, gold) in terms of the reactivity of the metals with water and dilute acids and that these reactions show the relative tendency of metal atoms to form cations	
4.4	Recall that: a most metals are extracted from ores found in the Earth's crust b unreactive metals are found in the Earth's crust as the uncombined elements	
4.5	Explain oxidation as the gain of oxygen and reduction as the loss of oxygen	
4.6	Recall that the extraction of metals involves reduction of ores	
4.7	Explain why the method used to extract a metal from its ore is related to its position in the reactivity series and the cost of the extraction process, illustrated by a heating with carbon (including iron) b electrolysis (including aluminium) (knowledge of the blast furnace is not required)	
4.8	**Evaluate alternative biological methods of metal extraction (bacterial and phytoextraction)**	
4.9	Explain how a metal's relative resistance to oxidation is related to its position in the reactivity series	
4.10	Evaluate the advantages of recycling metals, including economic implications and how recycling can preserve both the environment and the supply of valuable raw materials	
4.11	Describe that a life time assessment for a product involves consideration of the effect on the environment of obtaining the raw materials, manufacturing the product, using the product and disposing of the product when it is no longer useful	
4.12	Evaluate data from a life cycle assessment of a product	

Suggested practicals

- Investigate methods for extracting metals from their ores.
- Investigate simple oxidation and reduction reactions, such as burning elements in oxygen or competition reactions between metals and metal oxides.

Reversible reactions and equilibria

Students should:		Maths skills
4.13	Recall that chemical reactions are reversible, the use of the symbol ⇌ in equations and that the direction of some reversible reactions can be altered by changing the reaction conditions	
4.14	Explain what is meant by dynamic equilibrium	
4.15	Describe the formation of ammonia as a reversible reaction between nitrogen (extracted from the air) and hydrogen (obtained from natural gas) and that it can reach a dynamic equilibrium	
4.16	Recall the conditions for the Haber process as: a temperature 450 °C b pressure 200 atmospheres c iron catalyst	
4.17	**Predict how the position of a dynamic equilibrium is affected by changes in:** **a temperature** **b pressure** **c concentration**	

Suggested practicals

- Investigate simple reversible reactions, such as the decomposition of ammonium chloride.

The following topic is only found in the GCSE in Chemistry:

Topic 5 – Separate chemistry 1

Topics for Paper 4

Topic 6 – Groups in the periodic table

Group 1

Students should:		Maths skills
6.1	Explain why some elements can be classified as alkali metals (group 1), halogens (group 7) or noble gases (group 0), based on their position in the periodic table	
6.2	Recall that alkali metals a are soft b have relatively low melting points	
6.3	Describe the reactions of lithium, sodium and potassium with water	
6.4	Describe the pattern in reactivity of the alkali metals, lithium, sodium and potassium, with water; and use this pattern to predict the reactivity of other alkali metals	
6.5	Explain this pattern in reactivity in terms of electronic configurations	

Group 7

Students should:		Maths skills
6.6	Recall the colours and physical states of chlorine, bromine and iodine at room temperature	
6.7	Describe the pattern in the physical properties of the halogens, chlorine, bromine and iodine, and use this pattern to predict the physical properties of other halogens	1d 2c
6.8	Describe the chemical test for chlorine	
6.9	Describe the reactions of the halogens, chlorine, bromine and iodine, with metals to form metal halides, and use this pattern to predict the reactions of other halogens	
6.10	Recall that the halogens, chlorine, bromine and iodine, form hydrogen halides which dissolve in water to form acidic solutions, and use this pattern to predict the reactions of other halogens	
6.11	Describe the relative reactivity of the halogens chlorine, bromine and iodine, as shown by their displacement reactions with halide ions in aqueous solution, and use this pattern to predict the reactions of astatine	
6.12	**Explain why these displacement reactions are redox reactions in terms of gain and loss of electrons, identifying which of these are oxidised and which are reduced**	
6.13	Explain the relative reactivity of the halogens in terms of electronic configurations	

Group 0

Students should:	Maths skills
6.14 Explain why the noble gases are chemically inert, compared with the other elements, in terms of their electronic configurations	
6.15 Explain how the uses of noble gases depend on their inertness, low density and/or non-flammability	
6.16 Describe the pattern in the physical properties of some noble gases and use this pattern to predict the physical properties of other noble gases	1d 2c

Suggested practicals

- Investigate displacement reactions of halogens reacting with halide ions in solution.

Topic 7 – Rates of reaction and energy changes

Rates of reaction

Students should:		Maths skills
7.1	*Core Practical: Investigate the effects of changing the conditions of a reaction on the rates of chemical reactions by:* *a measuring the production of a gas (in the reaction between hydrochloric acid and marble chips)* *b observing a colour change (in the reaction between sodium thiosulfate and hydrochloric acid)*	1a, 1c 4a, 4b, 4c, 4d, 4e
7.2	Suggest practical methods for determining the rate of a given reaction	4b, 4c, 4d, 4e
7.3	Explain how reactions occur when particles collide and that rates of reaction are increased when the frequency and/or energy of collisions is increased	1c
7.4	Explain the effects on rates of reaction of changes in temperature, concentration, surface area to volume ratio of a solid and pressure (on reactions involving gases) in terms of frequency and/or energy of collisions between particles	1c, 1d 5c
7.5	Interpret graphs of mass, volume or concentration of reactant or product against time	1c 4a, 4d, 4e
7.6	Describe a catalyst as a substance that speeds up the rate of a reaction without altering the products of the reaction, being itself unchanged chemically and in mass at the end of the reaction	
7.7	Explain how the addition of a catalyst increases the rate of a reaction in terms of activation energy	
7.8	Recall that enzymes are biological catalysts and that enzymes are used in the production of alcoholic drinks	

Use of mathematics

- Arithmetic computation, ratio when measuring rates of reaction (1a and 1c).
- Drawing and interpreting appropriate graphs from data to determine rate of reaction (4b and 4c).
- Determining gradients of graphs as a measure of rate of change to determine rate (4d and **4e**).
- Proportionality when comparing factors affecting rate of reaction (1c).

Suggested practicals

- Investigate the effect of potential catalysts on the rate of decomposition of hydrogen peroxide.

Heat energy changes in chemical reactions

Students should:		Maths skills
7.9	Recall that changes in heat energy accompany the following changes: a salts dissolving in water b neutralisation reactions c displacement reactions d precipitation reactions and that, when these reactions take place in solution, temperature changes can be measured to reflect the heat changes	
7.10	Describe an exothermic change or reaction as one in which heat energy is given out	
7.11	Describe an endothermic change or reaction as one in which heat energy is taken in	
7.12	Recall that the breaking of bonds is endothermic and the making of bonds is exothermic	
7.13	Recall that the overall heat energy change for a reaction is: a exothermic if more heat energy is released in forming bonds in the products than is required in breaking bonds in the reactants b endothermic if less heat energy is released in forming bonds in the products than is required in breaking bonds in the reactants	
7.14	**Calculate the energy change in a reaction given the energies of bonds (in kJ mol^{-1})**	1a, 1c
7.15	Explain the term activation energy	
7.16	Draw and label reaction profiles for endothermic and exothermic reactions, identifying activation energy	4a

Use of mathematics

- Arithmetic computation when calculating energy changes (1a).
- Interpretation of charts and graphs when dealing with reaction profiles (4a).

Suggested practicals

- Measure temperature changes accompanying some of the following types of change:
  - a salts dissolving in water
  - b neutralisation reactions
  - c displacement reactions
  - d precipitation reactions.

Topic 8 – Fuels and Earth science

Fuels

Students should:		Maths skills
8.1	Recall that hydrocarbons are compounds that contain carbon and hydrogen only	
8.2	Describe crude oil as: a a complex mixture of hydrocarbons b containing molecules in which carbon atoms are in chains or rings (names, formulae and structures of specific ring molecules not required) c an important source of useful substances (fuels and feedstock for the petrochemical industry) d a finite resource	
8.3	Describe and explain the separation of crude oil into simpler, more useful mixtures by the process of fractional distillation	
8.4	Recall the names and uses of the following fractions: a gases, used in domestic heating and cooking b petrol, used as fuel for cars c kerosene, used as fuel for aircraft d diesel oil, used as fuel for some cars and trains e fuel oil, used as fuel for large ships and in some power stations f bitumen, used to surface roads and roofs	
8.5	Explain how hydrocarbons in different fractions differ from each other in: a the number of carbon and hydrogen atoms their molecules contain b boiling points c ease of ignition d viscosity and are mostly members of the alkane homologous series	4a, 4c
8.6	Explain an homologous series as a series of compounds which: a have the same general formula b differ by CH_2 in molecular formulae from neighbouring compounds c show a gradual variation in physical properties, as exemplified by their boiling points d have similar chemical properties	1c, 1d 4a

Students should:		Maths skills
8.7	Describe the complete combustion of hydrocarbon fuels as a reaction in which: a carbon dioxide and water are produced b energy is given out	
8.8	Explain why the incomplete combustion of hydrocarbons can produce carbon and carbon monoxide	
8.9	Explain how carbon monoxide behaves as a toxic gas	
8.10	Describe the problems caused by incomplete combustion producing carbon monoxide and soot in appliances that use carbon compounds as fuels	
8.11	Explain how impurities in some hydrocarbon fuels result in the production of sulfur dioxide	
8.12	Explain some problems associated with acid rain caused when sulfur dioxide dissolves in rain water	
8.13	Explain why, when fuels are burned in engines, oxygen and nitrogen can react together at high temperatures to produce oxides of nitrogen, which are pollutants	
8.14	Evaluate the advantages and disadvantages of using hydrogen, rather than petrol, as a fuel in cars	
8.15	Recall that petrol, kerosene and diesel oil are non-renewable fossil fuels obtained from crude oil and methane is a non-renewable fossil fuel found in natural gas	
8.16	Explain why cracking involves the breaking down of larger, saturated hydrocarbon molecules (alkanes) into smaller, more useful ones, some of which are unsaturated (alkenes)	1c
8.17	Explain why cracking is necessary	2c

Suggested practicals

- Investigate the fractional distillation of synthetic crude oil and the ease of ignition and viscosity of the fractions.
- Investigate the products produced from the complete combustion of a hydrocarbon.
- Investigate the cracking of paraffin oil.

Earth and atmospheric science

Students should:		Maths skills
8.18	Recall that the gases produced by volcanic activity formed the Earth's early atmosphere	
8.19	Describe that the Earth's early atmosphere was thought to contain: a little or no oxygen b a large amount of carbon dioxide c water vapour d small amounts of other gases and interpret evidence relating to this	2c 3a 4a
8.20	Explain how condensation of water vapour formed oceans	
8.21	Explain how the amount of carbon dioxide in the atmosphere was decreased when carbon dioxide dissolved as the oceans formed	
8.22	Explain how the growth of primitive plants used carbon dioxide and released oxygen by photosynthesis and consequently the amount of oxygen in the atmosphere gradually increased	
8.23	Describe the chemical test for oxygen	
8.24	Describe how various gases in the atmosphere, including carbon dioxide, methane and water vapour, absorb heat radiated from the Earth, subsequently releasing energy which keeps the Earth warm: this is known as the greenhouse effect	
8.25	Evaluate the evidence for human activity causing climate change, considering: a the correlation between the change in atmospheric carbon dioxide concentration, the consumption of fossil fuels and temperature change b the uncertainties caused by the location where these measurements are taken and historical accuracy	2c, 2h 4a
8.26	Describe: a the potential effects on the climate of increased levels of carbon dioxide and methane generated by human activity, including burning fossil fuels and livestock farming b that these effects may be mitigated: consider scale, risk and environmental implications	

Use of mathematics

- Extract and interpret information from charts, graphs and tables (2c and 4a).
- Use orders of magnitude to evaluate the significance of data (2h).

Suggested practicals

- Investigate the proportion of oxygen in the atmosphere.
- Investigate the presence of water vapour and carbon dioxide in the atmosphere.
- Investigate the volume of air used up and products formed when candles are burned.
- Carry out the test for oxygen.

The following topic is only found in the GCSE in Chemistry:

- Topic 9 – Separate chemistry 2.

Physics

Topics common to Paper 5 and Paper 6

Topic 1 – Key concepts of physics

Students should:		Maths skills
1.1	Recall and use the SI unit for physical quantities, as listed in *Appendix 5*	
1.2	Recall and use multiples and sub-multiples of units, including giga (G), mega (M), kilo (k), centi (c), milli (m), micro (μ) and nano (n)	3c
1.3	Be able to convert between different units, including hours to seconds	1c
1.4	Use significant figures and standard form where appropriate	1b

Use of mathematics

- Make calculations using ratios and proportional reasoning to convert units and to compute rates (1c, 3c).

Topics for Paper 5

Topic 2 – Motion and forces

Students should:		Maths skills
2.1	Explain that a scalar quantity has magnitude (size) but no specific direction	
2.2	Explain that a vector quantity has both magnitude (size) and a specific direction	5b
2.3	Explain the difference between vector and scalar quantities	5b
2.4	Recall vector and scalar quantities, including: a displacement/distance b velocity/speed c acceleration d force e weight/mass f momentum g energy	
2.5	Recall that velocity is speed in a stated direction	5b
2.6	Recall and use the equations: a (average) speed (metre per second, m/s) = distance (metre, m) ÷ time (s) b distance travelled (metre, m) = average speed (metre per second, m/s) × time (s)	1a, 1c, 1d 2a 3a, 3c, 3d
2.7	Analyse distance/time graphs including determination of speed from the gradient	2a 4a, 4b, 4d, 4e
2.8	Recall and use the equation: acceleration (metre per second squared, m/s^2) = change in velocity (metre per second, m/s) ÷ time taken (second, s) $a = \frac{(v - u)}{t}$	1a, 1c, 1d 2a 3a, 3b, 3c, 3d
2.9	Use the equation: (final velocity)^2 ((metre/second)^2, (m/s)^2) – (initial velocity)^2 ((metre/second)^2, (m/s)^2) = 2 × acceleration (metre per second squared, m/s^2) × distance (metre, m) $v^2 - u^2 = 2 \times a \times x$	1a, 1c, 1d 2a 3a, 3c, 3d

Students should:	Maths skills
2.10 Analyse velocity/time graphs to:	1a, 1c, 1d
a compare acceleration from gradients qualitatively	2a
b calculate the acceleration from the gradient (for uniform acceleration only)	4a, 4b, 4c, 4d, 4e, 4f
c determine the distance travelled using the area between the graph line and the time axis (for uniform acceleration only)	5c
2.11 Describe a range of laboratory methods for determining the speeds of objects such as the use of light gates	1a, 1d 2a, 2b, 2c, 2f, 2h 3a, 3c, 3d 4a, 4c
2.12 Recall some typical speeds encountered in everyday experience for wind and sound, and for walking, running, cycling and other transportation systems	
2.13 Recall that the acceleration, g, in free fall is 10 m/s^2 and be able to estimate the magnitudes of everyday accelerations	1d 2h
2.14 Recall Newton's first law and use it in the following situations:	1a, 1d
a where the resultant force on a body is zero, i.e. the body is moving at a constant velocity or is at rest	2a 3a, 3c, 3d
b where the resultant force is not zero, i.e. the speed and/or direction of the body change(s)	
2.15 Recall and use Newton's second law as: force (newton, N) = mass (kilogram, kg) × acceleration (metre per second squared, m/s^2) $F = m \times a$	1a, 1c, 1d 2a 3a, 3b, 3c, 3d
2.16 Define weight, recall and use the equation: weight (newton, N) = mass (kilogram, kg) × gravitational field strength (newton per kilogram, N/kg) $W = m \times g$	1a, 1c, 1d 2a 3a, 3b, 3c, 3d
2.17 Describe how weight is measured	
2.18 Describe the relationship between the weight of a body and the gravitational field strength	1c,
2.19 *Core Practical: Investigate the relationship between force, mass and acceleration by varying the masses added to trolleys*	1a, 1c,1d 2a, 2b, 2f 3a, 3b, 3c, 3d 4a, 4b, 4c, 4d
2.20 **Explain that an object moving in a circular orbit at constant speed has a changing velocity (qualitative only)**	5b

Students should:		Maths skills
2.21	**Explain that for motion in a circle there must be a resultant force known as a centripetal force that acts towards the centre of the circle**	5b
2.22	**Explain that inertial mass is a measure of how difficult it is to change the velocity of an object (including from rest) and know that it is defined as the ratio of force over acceleration**	1c
2.23	Recall and apply Newton's third law **both** to equilibrium situations **and to collision interactions and relate it to the conservation of momentum in collisions**	1a, 1c, 1d 2a 3a, 3b, 3c, 3d
2.24	**Define momentum, recall and use the equation:** **momentum (kilogram metre per second, kg m/s) = mass (kilogram, kg) × velocity (metre per second, m/s)** $p = m \times v$	1a, 1c, 1d 2a 3a, 3b, 3c, 3d
2.25	**Describe examples of momentum in collisions**	1a, 1c, 1d 2a 3a, 3b, 3c, 3d
2.26	**Use Newton's second law as:** **force (newton, N) = change in momentum (kilogram metre per second, kg m/s) ÷ time (second, s)** $F = \frac{(mv - mu)}{t}$	1a, 1c, 1d 2a 3a, 3b, 3c, 3d
2.27	Explain methods of measuring human reaction times and recall typical results	2a, 2b, 2c, 2g
2.28	Recall that the stopping distance of a vehicle is made up of the sum of the thinking distance and the braking distance	1a
2.29	Explain that the stopping distance of a vehicle is affected by a range of factors including: a the mass of the vehicle b the speed of the vehicle c the driver's reaction time d the state of the vehicle's brakes e the state of the road f the amount of friction between the tyre and the road surface	1c, 1d 2b, 2c, 2h 3b, 3c
2.30	Describe the factors affecting a driver's reaction time including drugs and distractions	1d 2h

Students should:	Maths skills
2.31 Explain the dangers caused by large decelerations **and estimate the forces involved in typical situations on a public road**	1d 2b, 2h 3c

Specification points 2.32 and 2.33 are in the GCSE in Physics only.

Use of mathematics

- Make calculations using ratios and proportional reasoning to convert units and to compute rates (1c, 3c).
- Relate changes and differences in motion to appropriate distance-time, and velocity-time graphs, and interpret lines and slopes (4a, 4b, 4c, 4d).
- **Interpret enclosed areas in velocity-time graphs (4a, 4b, 4c, 4d, 4f).**
- Apply formulae relating distance, time and speed, for uniform motion, and for motion with uniform acceleration, and calculate average speed for non-uniform motion (1a, 1c, 2b, 3c).

Suggested practicals

- Investigate the acceleration, g, in free fall and the magnitudes of everyday accelerations.
- Investigate conservation of momentum during collisions.
- Investigate inelastic collisions with the two objects remaining together after the collision and also 'near' elastic collisions.
- Investigate the relationship between mass and weight.
- Investigate how crumple zones can be used to reduce the forces in collisions.

Topic 3 – Conservation of energy

Students should:		Maths skills
3.1	Recall and use the equation to calculate the change in gravitational PE when an object is raised above the ground: change in gravitational potential energy (joule, J) = mass (kilogram, kg) × gravitational field strength (newton per kilogram, N/kg) × change in vertical height (metre, m) $\Delta GPE = m \times g \times \Delta h$	1a, 1c, 1d 2a 3a, 3b, 3c, 3d
3.2	Recall and use the equation to calculate the amounts of energy associated with a moving object: kinetic energy (joule, J) = $\frac{1}{2}$ × mass (kilogram, kg) × (speed)^2 ((metre/second)^2, (m/s)^2) $KE = \frac{1}{2} \times m \times v^2$	1a, 1c, 1d 2a 3a, 3b, 3c, 3d
3.3	Draw and interpret diagrams to represent energy transfers	1c 2c
3.4	Explain what is meant by conservation of energy	
3.5	Analyse the changes involved in the way energy is stored when a system changes, including: a an object projected upwards or up a slope b a moving object hitting an obstacle c an object being accelerated by a constant force d a vehicle slowing down e bringing water to a boil in an electric kettle	
3.6	Explain that where there are energy transfers in a closed system there is no net change to the total energy in that system	
3.7	Explain that mechanical processes become wasteful when they cause a rise in temperature so dissipating energy in heating the surroundings	
3.8	Explain, using examples, how in all system changes energy is dissipated so that it is stored in less useful ways	
3.9	Explain ways of reducing unwanted energy transfer including through lubrication, thermal insulation	
3.10	Describe the effects of the thickness and thermal conductivity of the walls of a building on its rate of cooling qualitatively	
3.11	Recall and use the equation: $\text{efficiency} = \frac{\text{(useful energy transferred by the device)}}{\text{(total energy supplied to the device)}}$	1a, 1c, 1d 2a 3a, 3b, 3c, 3d
3.12	**Explain how efficiency can be increased**	

Students should:		Maths skills
3.13	Describe the main energy sources available for use on Earth (including fossil fuels, nuclear fuel, bio-fuel, wind, hydro-electricity, the tides and the Sun), and compare the ways in which both renewable and non-renewable sources are used	2c, 2g
3.14	Explain patterns and trends in the use of energy resources	2c, 2g

Use of mathematics

- Make calculations using ratios and proportional reasoning to convert units and to compute rates (1c, 3c).
- Calculate relevant values of stored energy and energy transfers; convert between newton-metres and joules (1c, 3c).
- Make calculations of the energy changes associated with changes in a system, recalling or selecting the relevant equations for mechanical, electrical, and thermal processes; thereby express in quantitative form and on a common scale the overall redistribution of energy in the system (1a, 1c, 3c).

Suggested practicals

- Investigate conservation of energy.

Topic 4 – Waves

Students should:		Maths skills
4.1	Recall that waves transfer energy and information without transferring matter	
4.2	Describe evidence that with water and sound waves it is the wave and not the water or air itself that travels	
4.3	Define and use the terms frequency and wavelength as applied to waves	
4.4	Use the terms, amplitude, period and wave velocity as applied to waves	
4.5	Describe the difference between longitudinal and transverse waves by referring to sound, electromagnetic, seismic and water waves	
4.6	Recall and use both the equations below for all waves: wave speed (metre/second, m/s) = frequency (hertz, Hz) × wavelength (metre, m) $v = f \times \lambda$ wave speed (metre/second, m/s) = distance (metre, m) ÷ time (second, s) $v = \frac{x}{t}$	1a, 1b, 1c, 1d 2a 3a, 3b, 3c, 3d
4.7	Describe how to measure the velocity of sound in air and ripples on water surfaces	2g
4.10	Explain how waves will be refracted at a boundary in terms of the change of direction **and speed**	1c 3c 5b
4.11	**Recall that different substances may absorb, transmit, refract or reflect waves in ways that vary with wavelength**	
4.17	*Core Practical: Investigate the suitability of equipment to measure the speed, frequency and wavelength of a wave in a solid and a fluid*	2g

Specification points 4.8, 4.9, 4.12, 4.13, 4.14, 4.15 and 4.16 are in the GCSE in Physics only.

Use of mathematics

- Make calculations using ratios and proportional reasoning to convert units and to compute rates (1c, 3c).
- Apply formulae relating velocity, frequency and wavelength (1c, 3c).

Suggested practicals

- Investigate models to show refraction, such as toy cars travelling into a region of sand.
- Investigate refraction in rectangular glass blocks.

Topic 5 – Light and the electromagnetic spectrum

Students should:		Maths skills
5.7	Recall that all electromagnetic waves are transverse, that they travel at the same speed in a vacuum	
5.8	Explain, with examples, that all electromagnetic waves transfer energy from source to observer	
5.9	*Investigate refraction in rectangular glass blocks in terms of the interaction of electromagnetic waves with matter*	
5.10	Recall the main groupings of the continuous electromagnetic spectrum including (in order) radio waves, microwaves, infrared, visible (including the colours of the visible spectrum), ultraviolet, x-rays and gamma rays	
5.11	Describe the electromagnetic spectrum as continuous from radio waves to gamma rays and that the radiations within it can be grouped in order of decreasing wavelength and increasing frequency	1a, 1c 3c
5.12	Recall that our eyes can only detect a limited range of frequencies of electromagnetic radiation	
5.13	**Recall that different substances may absorb, transmit, refract or reflect electromagnetic waves in ways that vary with wavelength**	
5.14	**Explain the effects of differences in the velocities of electromagnetic waves in different substances**	1a, 1c 3c
5.20	Recall that the potential danger associated with an electromagnetic wave increases with increasing frequency	
5.21	Describe the harmful effects on people of excessive exposure to electromagnetic radiation, including: a microwaves: internal heating of body cells b infrared: skin burns c ultraviolet: damage to surface cells and eyes, leading to skin cancer and eye conditions d x-rays and gamma rays: mutation or damage to cells in the body	

Students should:	Maths skills
5.22 Describe some uses of electromagnetic radiation a radio waves: including broadcasting, communications and satellite transmissions b microwaves: including cooking, communications and satellite transmissions c infrared: including cooking, thermal imaging, short range communications, optical fibres, television remote controls and security systems d visible light: including vision, photography and illumination e ultraviolet: including security marking, fluorescent lamps, detecting forged bank notes and disinfecting water f x-rays: including observing the internal structure of objects, airport security scanners and medical x-rays g gamma rays: including sterilising food and medical equipment, and the detection of cancer and its treatment	
5.23 **Recall that radio waves can be produced by, or can themselves induce, oscillations in electrical circuits**	
5.24 Recall that changes in atoms and nuclei can a generate radiations over a wide frequency range b be caused by absorption of a range of radiations	

Specification points 5.1, 5.2, 5.3, 5.4, 5.5, 5.6, 5.15, 5.16, 5.17, 5.18 and 5.19 are in the GCSE in Physics only.

Use of mathematics

- Make calculations using ratios and proportional reasoning to convert units and to compute rates (1c, 3c).
- Apply the relationships between frequency and wavelength across the electromagnetic spectrum (1a, 1c, 3c).

Suggested practicals

- Construct a simple spectrometer, from a CD or DVD, and use it to analyse common light sources.
- Investigate the areas beyond the visible spectrum, such as the work of Herschel and Ritter in discovering IR and UV respectively.

Topic 6 – Radioactivity

Students should:		Maths skills
6.1	Describe an atom as a positively charged nucleus, consisting of protons and neutrons, surrounded by negatively charged electrons, with the nuclear radius much smaller than that of the atom and with almost all of the mass in the nucleus	5b
6.2	Recall the typical size (order of magnitude) of atoms and small molecules	
6.3	Describe the structure of nuclei of isotopes using the terms atomic (proton) number and mass (nucleon) number and using symbols in the format using symbols in the format $^{13}_{6}C$	1a 3a
6.4	Recall that the nucleus of each element has a characteristic positive charge, but that isotopes of an element differ in mass by having different numbers of neutrons	2g 5b
6.5	Recall the relative masses and relative electric charges of protons, neutrons, electrons and positrons	
6.6	Recall that in an atom the number of protons equals the number of electrons and is therefore neutral	
6.7	Recall that in each atom its electrons orbit the nucleus at different set distances from the nucleus	5b
6.8	Explain that electrons change orbit when there is absorption or emission of electromagnetic radiation	5b
6.9	Explain how atoms may form positive ions by losing outer electrons	5b
6.10	Recall that alpha, β– (beta minus), β+ (positron), gamma rays and neutron radiation are emitted from unstable nuclei in a random process	
6.11	Recall that alpha, β– (beta minus), β+ (positron) and gamma rays are ionising radiations	
6.12	Explain what is meant by background radiation	
6.13	Describe the origins of background radiation from Earth and space	
6.14	Describe methods for measuring and detecting radioactivity limited to photographic film and a Geiger–Müller tube	
6.15	Recall that an alpha particle is equivalent to a helium nucleus, a beta particle is an electron emitted from the nucleus and a gamma ray is electromagnetic radiation	
6.16	Compare alpha, beta and gamma radiations in terms of their abilities to penetrate and ionise	

Students should:		Maths skills
6.17	Describe how and why the atomic model has changed over time including reference to the plum pudding model and Rutherford alpha particle scattering leading to the Bohr model	5b
6.18	Describe the process of β− decay (a neutron becomes a proton plus an electron)	1b, 1c 3c
6.19	Describe the process of β+ decay (a proton becomes a neutron plus a positron)	1b, 1c 3c
6.20	Explain the effects on the atomic (proton) number and mass (nucleon) number of radioactive decays (α, β, γ and neutron emission)	1b, 1c 3c
6.21	Recall that nuclei that have undergone radioactive decay often undergo nuclear rearrangement with a loss of energy as gamma radiation	
6.22	Use given data to balance nuclear equations in terms of mass and charge	1b, 1c 3c
6.23	Describe how the activity of a radioactive source decreases over a period of time	2g 4c
6.24	Recall that the unit of activity of a radioactive isotope is the Becquerel, Bq	
6.25	Explain that the half-life of a radioactive isotope is the time taken for half the undecayed nuclei to decay or the activity of a source to decay by half	1c, 1d 2a
6.26	Explain that it cannot be predicted when a particular nucleus will decay but half-life enables the activity of a very large number of nuclei to be predicted during the decay process	1c 3d
6.27	Use the concept of half-life to carry out simple calculations on the decay of a radioactive isotope, including graphical representations	1a, 1b, 1c, 1d 2a, 2g 3a, 3b, 3c, 3d
6.29	Describe the dangers of ionising radiation in terms of tissue damage and possible mutations and relate this to the precautions needed	
6.31	Explain the precautions taken to ensure the safety of people exposed to radiation, including limiting the dose for patients and the risks to medical personnel	
6.32	Describe the differences between contamination and irradiation effects and compare the hazards associated with these two	

Specification points 6.28, 6.30, 6.33, 6.34, 6.35, 6.36, 6.37, 6.38, 6.39, 6.40, 6.41, 6.42, 6.43, 6.44, 6.45 and 6.46 are in the GCSE in Physics only.

Use of mathematics

- Make calculations using ratios and proportional reasoning to convert units and to compute rates (1c, 3c).
- Balance equations representing alpha-, beta- or gamma-radiations in terms of the masses and charges of the atoms involved (1b, 1c, 3c).
- **Calculate the net decline, expressed as a ratio, in a radioactive emission after a given number of half-lives (1c, 3d).**

Suggested practicals

- Investigate models which simulate radioactive decay.

The following topics are only found in the GCSE in Physics:

Topic 7 – Astronomy

Topics for Paper 6

Topic 8 – Energy – forces doing work

Students should:		Maths skills
8.1	Describe the changes involved in the way energy is stored when systems change	
8.2	Draw and interpret diagrams to represent energy transfers	1c 2c
8.3	Explain that where there are energy transfers in a closed system there is no net change to the total energy in that system	
8.4	Identify the different ways that the energy of a system can be changed a through work done by forces b in electrical equipment c in heating	
8.5	Describe how to measure the work done by a force and understand that energy transferred (joule, J) is equal to work done (joule, J)	
8.6	Recall and use the equation: work done (joule, J) = force (newton, N) × distance moved in the direction of the force (metre, m) $E = F \times d$	1a, 1b, 1c, 1d 2a 3a, 3b, 3c, 3d 4f
8.7	Describe and calculate the changes in energy involved when a system is changed by work done by forces	
8.8	Recall and use the equation to calculate the change in gravitational PE when an object is raised above the ground: change in gravitational potential energy (joule, J) = mass (kilogram, kg) × gravitational field strength (newton per kilogram, N/kg) × change in vertical height (metre, m) $\Delta GPE = m \times g \times \Delta h$	1a, 1c, 1d 2a 3a, 3b, 3c, 3d
8.9	Recall and use the equation to calculate the amounts of energy associated with a moving object: kinetic energy (joule, J) = $\frac{1}{2}$ × mass (kilogram, kg) × (speed)^2 ((metre/second)^2, (m/s)^2) $KE = \frac{1}{2} \times m \times v^2$	1a, 1c, 1d 2a 3a, 3b, 3c, 3d
8.10	Explain, using examples, how in all system changes energy is dissipated so that it is stored in less useful ways	

Students should:		Maths skills
8.11	Explain that mechanical processes become wasteful when they cause a rise in temperature so dissipating energy in heating the surroundings	
8.12	Define power as the rate at which energy is transferred and use examples to explain this definition	1c
8.13	Recall and use the equation: power (watt, W) = work done (joule, J) ÷ time taken (second, s) $P = \frac{E}{t}$	1a, 1c, 1d 2a 3a, 3b, 3c, 3d
8.14	Recall that one watt is equal to one joule per second, J/s	1c
8.15	Recall and use the equation: $\text{efficiency} = \frac{(\text{useful energy transferred by the device})}{(\text{total energy supplied to the device})}$	1a, 1c, 1d 2a 3a, 3b, 3c, 3d

Use of mathematics

- Make calculations using ratios and proportional reasoning to convert units and to compute rates (1c, 3c).
- Make calculations of the energy changes associated with changes in a system, recalling or selecting the relevant equations for mechanical, electrical, and thermal processes; thereby express in quantitative form and on a common scale the overall redistribution of energy in the system (1a, 1c, 3c).
- Calculate relevant values of stored energy and energy transfers; convert between newton-metres and joules (1c, 3c).

Suggested practicals

- Investigate power by running up the stairs or lifting objects of different weights.

Topic 9 – Forces and their effects

Students should:		Maths skills
9.1	Describe, with examples, how objects can interact a at a distance without contact, linking these to the gravitational, electrostatic and magnetic fields involved b by contact, including normal contact force and friction c producing pairs of forces which can be represented as vectors	
9.2	Explain the difference between vector and scalar quantities using examples	
9.3	**Use vector diagrams to illustrate resolution of forces, a net force, and equilibrium situations (scale drawings only)**	4a 5a, 5b
9.4	**Draw and use free body force diagrams**	4a 5a, 5b
9.5	**Explain examples of the forces acting on an isolated solid object or a system where several forces lead to a resultant force on an object and the special case of balanced forces when the resultant force is zero**	5a
9.10	Explain ways of reducing unwanted energy transfer through lubrication	

Specification points 9.6, 9.7, 9.8 and 9.9 are in the GCSE in Physics only.

Use of mathematics

- Make calculations using ratios and proportional reasoning to convert units and to compute rates (1c, 3c).
- **Use vector diagrams to illustrate resolution of forces, a net force, and equilibrium situations (scale drawings only) (4a, 5a, 5b).**

Topic 10 – Electricity and circuits

Students should:		Maths skills
10.1	Describe the structure of the atom, limited to the position, mass and charge of protons, neutrons and electrons	5b
10.2	Draw and use electric circuit diagrams representing them with the conventions of positive and negative terminals, and the symbols that represent cells, including batteries, switches, voltmeters, ammeters, resistors, variable resistors, lamps, motors, diodes, thermistors, LDRs and LEDs	5b
10.3	Describe the differences between series and parallel circuits	
10.4	Recall that a voltmeter is connected in parallel with a component to measure the potential difference (voltage), in volt, across it	
10.5	Explain that potential difference (voltage) is the energy transferred per unit charge passed and hence that the volt is a joule per coulomb	1a, 1c 3c
10.6	Recall and use the equation: energy transferred (joule, J) = charge moved (coulomb, C) × potential difference (volt, V) $E = Q \times V$	1a, 1b, 1c, 1d 2a 3a, 3b, 3c, 3d
10.7	Recall that an ammeter is connected in series with a component to measure the current, in amp, in the component	
10.8	Explain that an electric current as the rate of flow of charge and the current in metals is a flow of electrons	
10.9	Recall and use the equation: charge (coulomb, C) = current (ampere, A) × time (second, s) $Q = I \times t$	1a, 1b, 1c, 1d 2a 3a, 3b, 3c, 3d
10.10	Describe that when a closed circuit includes a source of potential difference there will be a current in the circuit	
10.11	Recall that current is conserved at a junction in a circuit	
10.12	Explain how changing the resistance in a circuit changes the current and how this can be achieved using a variable resistor	
10.13	Recall and use the equation: potential difference (volt, V) = current (ampere, A) × resistance (ohm, Ω) $V = I \times R$	1a, 1d 2a 3a, 3c, 3d
10.14	Explain why, if two resistors are in series, the net resistance is increased, whereas with two in parallel the net resistance is decreased	

Students should:	Maths skills
10.15 Calculate the currents, potential differences and resistances in series circuits	1a, 1d 2a 3a, 3c, 3d
10.16 Explain the design and construction of series circuits for testing and measuring	
10.17 *Core Practical: Construct electrical circuits to:* *a investigate the relationship between potential difference, current and resistance for a resistor and a filament lamp* *b test series and parallel circuits using resistors and filament lamps*	1a, 1c, 1d 2a, 2b, 2f 3a, 3b, 3c, 3d 4a, 4b, 4c, 4d, 4e
10.18 Explain how current varies with potential difference for the following devices and how this relates to resistance a filament lamps b diodes c fixed resistors	2g 4a, 4b, 4c, 4d, 4e
10.19 Describe how the resistance of a light-dependent resistor (LDR) varies with light intensity	4c, 4d
10.20 Describe how the resistance of a thermistor varies with change of temperature (negative temperature coefficient thermistors only)	4c, 4d
10.21 Explain how the design and use of circuits can be used to explore the variation of resistance in the following devices a filament lamps b diodes c thermistors d LDRs	5b
10.22 Recall that, when there is an electric current in a resistor, there is an energy transfer which heats the resistor	
10.23 Explain that electrical energy is dissipated as thermal energy in the surroundings when an electrical current does work against electrical resistance	
10.24 Explain the energy transfer (in 10.22 above) as the result of collisions between electrons and the ions in the lattice	
10.25 **Explain ways of reducing unwanted energy transfer through low resistance wires**	
10.26 Describe the advantages and disadvantages of the heating effect of an electric current	

Students should:	Maths skills
10.27 Use the equation: energy transferred (joule, J) = current (ampere, A) × potential difference (volt, V) × time (second, s) $E = I \times V \times t$	1a, 1b, 1c, 1d 2a 3a, 3b, 3c, 3d
10.28 Describe power as the energy transferred per second and recall that it is measured in watt	1c
10.29 Recall and use the equation: power (watt, W) = energy transferred (joule, J) ÷ time taken (second, s) $P = \frac{E}{t}$	1a, 1b, 1c, 1d 2a 3a, 3b, 3c, 3d
10.30 Explain how the power transfer in any circuit device is related to the potential difference across it and the current in it	1a, 1c, 1d 2a 3a, 3b, 3c, 3d
10.31 Recall and use the equations: electrical power (watt, W) = current (ampere, A) × potential difference (volt, V) $P = I \times V$ electrical power (watt, W) = current squared (ampere^2, A^2) × resistance (ohm, Ω) $P = I^2 \times R$	1a, 1b, 1c, 1d 2a 3a, 3b, 3c, 3d
10.32 Describe how, in different domestic devices, energy is transferred from batteries and the a.c. mains to the energy of motors and heating devices	
10.33 Explain the difference between direct and alternating voltage	4c
10.34 Describe direct current (d.c.) as movement of charge in one direction only and recall that cells and batteries supply direct current (d.c.)	
10.35 Describe that in alternating current (a.c.) the movement of charge changes direction	
10.36 Recall that in the UK the domestic supply is a.c., at a frequency of 50 Hz and a voltage of about 230 V	
10.37 Explain the difference in function between the live and the neutral mains input wires	
10.38 Explain the function of an earth wire and of fuses or circuit breakers in ensuring safety	
10.39 Explain why switches and fuses should be connected in the live wire of a domestic circuit	

Students should:	Maths skills
10.40 Recall the potential differences between the live, neutral and earth mains wires	
10.41 Explain the dangers of providing any connection between the live wire and earth	
10.42 Describe, with examples, the relationship between the power ratings for domestic electrical appliances and the changes in stored energy when they are in use	1c 2c

Use of mathematics

- Make calculations using ratios and proportional reasoning to convert units and to compute rates (1c, 3c).
- Apply the equations relating p.d., current, quantity of charge, resistance, power, energy, and time, and solve problems for circuits which include resistors in series, using the concept of equivalent resistance (1c, 3b, 3c, 3d).
- Use graphs to explore whether circuit elements are linear or non-linear and relate the curves produced to their function and properties (4c, 4d).
- Make calculations of the energy changes associated with changes in a system, recalling or selecting the relevant equations for mechanical, electrical, and thermal processes; thereby express in quantitative form and on a common scale the overall redistribution of energy in the system (1a, 1c, 3c).

Suggested practicals

- Investigate the power consumption of low-voltage electrical items.

The following topic is only found in the GCSE in Physics:

Topic 11 – Static electricity.

Topic 12 – Magnetism and the motor effect

Students should:		Maths skills
12.1	Recall that unlike magnetic poles attract and like magnetic poles repel	
12.2	Describe the uses of permanent and temporary magnetic materials including cobalt, steel, iron and nickel	
12.3	Explain the difference between permanent and induced magnets	
12.4	Describe the shape and direction of the magnetic field around bar magnets and for a uniform field, and relate the strength of the field to the concentration of lines	5b
12.5	Describe the use of plotting compasses to show the shape and direction of the field of a magnet and the Earth's magnetic field	5b
12.6	Explain how the behaviour of a magnetic compass is related to evidence that the core of the Earth must be magnetic	5b
12.7	Describe how to show that a current can create a magnetic effect and relate the shape and direction of the magnetic field around a long straight conductor to the direction of the current	5b
12.8	Recall that the strength of the field depends on the size of the current and the distance from the long straight conductor	
12.9	Explain how inside a solenoid (an example of an electromagnet) the fields from individual coils a add together to form a very strong almost uniform field along the centre of the solenoid b cancel to give a weaker field outside the solenoid	5b
12.10	**Recall that a current carrying conductor placed near a magnet experiences a force and that an equal and opposite force acts on the magnet**	5b
12.11	**Explain that magnetic forces are due to interactions between magnetic fields**	
12.12	**Recall and use Fleming's left-hand rule to represent the relative directions of the force, the current and the magnetic field for cases where they are mutually perpendicular**	5b
12.13	**Use the equation:** **force on a conductor at right angles to a magnetic field carrying a current (newton, N) = magnetic flux density (tesla, T or newton per ampere metre, N/A m) × current (ampere, A) × length (metre, m)** $F = B \times I \times l$	1a, 1c, 1d 2a 3a, 3b, 3c, 3d

Specification point 12.14 is in the GCSE in Physics only.

Use of mathematics

- Make calculations using ratios and proportional reasoning to convert units and to compute rates (1c, 3c).

Suggested practicals

- Construct an electric motor.

Topic 13 – Electromagnetic induction

Students should:	Maths skills
13.2 **Recall the factors that affect the size and direction of an induced potential difference, and describe how the magnetic field produced opposes the original change**	5b
13.5 **Explain how an alternating current in one circuit can induce a current in another circuit in a transformer**	
13.6 **Recall that a transformer can change the size of an alternating voltage**	
13.8 Explain why, in the national grid, electrical energy is transferred at high voltages from power stations, and then transferred at lower voltages in each locality for domestic uses as it improves the efficiency by reducing heat loss in transmission lines	
13.9 Explain where and why step-up and step-down transformers are used in the transmission of electricity in the national grid	
13.10 Use the power equation (for transformers with100% efficiency): potential difference across primary coil (volt, V) × current in primary coil (ampere, A) = potential difference across secondary coil (volt, V) × current in secondary coil (ampere, A) $V_P \times I_P = V_S \times I_S$	1a, 1c, 1d 2a 3a, 3b, 3c, 3d

Specification points 13.1, 13.3, 13.4, 13.7 and 13.11 are in the GCSE in Physics only.

Use of mathematics

- Make calculations using ratios and proportional reasoning to convert units and to compute rates (1c, 3c).
- Make calculations of the energy changes associated with changes in a system, recalling or selecting the relevant equations for mechanical, electrical, and thermal processes; thereby express in quantitative form and on a common scale the overall redistribution of energy in the system (1a, 1c, 3c).

Suggested practicals

- Investigate factors affecting the generation of electric current by induction.

Topic 14 – Particle model

Students should:		Maths skills
14.1	Use a simple kinetic theory model to explain the different states of matter (solids, liquids and gases) in terms of the movement and arrangement of particles	
14.2	Recall and use the equation: density (kilogram per cubic metre, kg/m^3) = mass (kilogram, kg) ÷ volume (cubic metre, m^3) $\rho = \frac{m}{V}$	1a, 1b, 1c, 1d 2a 3a, 3b, 3c, 3d 5c
14.3	*Core Practical: Investigate the densities of solid and liquids*	1a, 1b, 1c, 1d 2a, 2c, 2f 3a, 3b, 3c, 3d 4a, 4c 5c
14.4	Explain the differences in density between the different states of matter in terms of the arrangements of the atoms or molecules	5b
14.5	Describe that when substances melt, freeze, evaporate, boil, condense or sublimate mass is conserved and that these physical changes differ from some chemical changes because the material recovers its original properties if the change is reversed	
14.6	Explain how heating a system will change the energy stored within the system and raise its temperature or produce changes of state	
14.7	Define the terms specific heat capacity and specific latent heat and explain the differences between them	
14.8	Use the equation: change in thermal energy (joule, J) = mass (kilogram, kg) × specific heat capacity (joule per kilogram degree Celsius, J/kg °C) × change in temperature (degree Celsius, °C) $\Delta Q = m \times c \times \Delta\theta$	1a, 1b, 1c, 1d 2a 3a, 3b, 3c, 3d
14.9	Use the equation: thermal energy for a change of state (joule , J) = mass (kilogram, kg) × specific latent heat (joule per kilogram, J/kg) $Q = m \times L$	1a, 1b, 1c, 1d 2a 3a, 3b, 3c, 3d
14.10	Explain ways of reducing unwanted energy transfer through thermal insulation	

Students should:	Maths skills
14.11 *Core Practical: Investigate the properties of water by determining the specific heat capacity of water and obtaining a temperature-time graph for melting ice*	1a, 1b, 1c, 1d 2a, 2b, 2f 3a, 3b, 3c, 3d 4a, 4c, 4e
14.12 Explain the pressure of a gas in terms of the motion of its particles	5b
14.13 Explain the effect of changing the temperature of a gas on the velocity of its particles and hence on the pressure produced by a fixed mass of gas at constant volume (qualitative only)	5b
14.14 Describe the term absolute zero, −273 °C, in terms of the lack of movement of particles	
14.15 Convert between the kelvin and Celsius scales	1a 2a

Specification points 14.16, 14.17, 14.18, 14.19 and 14.20 are in the GCSE in Physics only.

Use of mathematics

- Make calculations using ratios and proportional reasoning to convert units and to compute rates (1c, 3c).
- Make calculations of the energy changes associated with changes in a system, recalling or selecting the relevant equations for mechanical, electrical, and thermal processes; thereby express in quantitative form and on a common scale the overall redistribution of energy in the system (1a, 1c, 3c).
- Calculate relevant values of stored energy and energy transfers; convert between newton-metres and joules (1c, 3c).
- Apply the relationship between density, mass and volume to changes where mass is conserved (1a, 1b, 1c, 3c).
- Apply the relationship between change in internal energy of a material and its mass, specific heat capacity and temperature change to calculate the energy change involved; apply the relationship between specific latent heat and mass to calculate the energy change involved in a change of state (1a, 3c, 3d).

Suggested practicals

- Investigate the temperature and volume relationship for a gas.
- Investigate the volume and pressure relationship for a gas.
- Investigate latent heat of vaporisation.

Topic 15 – Forces and matter

Students should:		Maths skills
15.1	Explain, using springs and other elastic objects, that stretching, bending or compressing an object requires more than one force	
15.2	Describe the difference between elastic and inelastic distortion	
15.3	Recall and use the equation for linear elastic distortion including calculating the spring constant: force exerted on a spring (newton, N) = spring constant (newton per metre, N/m) × extension (metre, m) $F = k \times x$	1a, 1c, 1d 2a 3a, 3b, 3c, 3d
15.4	Use the equation to calculate the work done in stretching a spring: energy transferred in stretching (joule, J) = 0.5 × spring constant (newton per metre, N/m) × (extension (metre, m))^2 $E = \frac{1}{2} \times k \times x^2$	1a, 1c, 1d 2a 3a, 3b, 3c, 3d 4c, 4e, 4f
15.5	Describe the difference between linear and non-linear relationships between force and extension	4c, 4e
15.6	*Core Practical: Investigate the extension and work done when applying forces to a spring*	1a, 1c, 1d 2a, 2b, 2c, 2f 3a, 3b, 3c, 3d 4a, 4b, 4c, 4d

Specification points 15.7, 15.8, 15.9, 15.10, 15.11, 15.12, 15.13, 15.14, 15.15, 15.16 and 15.17 are in the GCSE in Physics only.

Use of mathematics

- Make calculations using ratios and proportional reasoning to convert units and to compute rates (1c, 3c).
- Calculate relevant values of stored energy and energy transfers; convert between newton-metres and joules (1c, 3c).
- Make calculations of the energy changes associated with changes in a system, recalling or selecting the relevant equations for mechanical, electrical, and thermal processes; thereby express in quantitative form and on a common scale the overall redistribution of energy in the system (1a, 1c, 3c).

Suggested practicals

- Investigate the stretching of rubber bands.

3 Assessment information

Common to Papers 1 to 6

- First assessment: May/June 2018.
- The assessment is 1 hour and 10 minutes.
- The assessment is out of 60 marks.
- The assessment consists of six questions.
- Students must answer all questions.
- The paper will include multiple-choice, short answer questions, calculations and extended open-response questions.
- Calculators may be used in the examination.
- Available at foundation tier and higher tier.
- Students must complete all assessments for this qualification in the same tier.
- The foundation tier paper will target grades 1–5.
- The higher tier paper will target grades 4–9.
- 16 marks of the paper will be overlap questions that appear in both the foundation and higher tier papers.

Paper 1: Biology 1 (Paper code: 1SC0/1BF, 1SC0/1BH)

Content assessed

Topic 1 – Key concepts in biology, Topic 2 – Cells and control, Topic 3 – Genetics, Topic 4 – Natural selection and genetic modification, Topic 5 – Health, disease and the development of medicines

Paper 2: Biology 2 (Paper code: 1SC0/2BF, 1SC0/2BH)

Content assessed

Topic 1 – Key concepts in biology, Topic 6 – Plant structures and their functions, Topic 7 – Animal coordination, control and homeostasis, Topic 8 – Exchange and transport in animals, Topic 9 – Ecosystems and material cycles

Paper 3: Chemistry 1 (Paper code: 1SC0/1CF, 1SC0/1CH)

Content assessed

Topic 1 – Key concepts in chemistry, Topic 2 – States of matter and mixtures, Topic 3 – Chemical changes, Topic 4 – Extracting metals and equilibria

Paper 4: Chemistry 2 (Paper code: 1SC0/2CF, 1SC0/2CH)

Content assessed

Topic 1 – Key concepts in chemistry, Topic 6 – Groups in the periodic table, Topic 7 – Rates of reaction and energy changes, Topic 8 – Fuels and Earth science

Paper 5: Physics 1 (Paper code: 1SC0/1PF, 1SC0/1PH)

Content assessed

Topic 1 – Key concepts of physics, Topic 2 – Motion and forces, Topic 3 – Conservation of energy, Topic 4 – Waves, Topic 5 – Light and the electromagnetic spectrum, Topic 6 – Radioactivity

Paper 6: Physics 2 (Paper code: 1SC0/2PF, 1SC0/2PH)

Content assessed

Topic 1 – Key concepts of physics, Topic 8 – Energy - Forces doing work, Topic 9 – Forces and their effects, Topic 10 – Electricity and circuits, Topic 12 – Magnetism and the motor effect, Topic 13 – Electromagnetic induction, Topic 14 – Particle model, Topic 15 – Forces and matter

Assessment Objectives

Students must:		% in GCSE
AO1	Demonstrate knowledge and understanding of: • scientific ideas • scientific techniques and procedures.	40
AO2	Apply knowledge and understanding of: • scientific ideas • scientific enquiry, techniques and procedures.	40
AO3	Analyse information and ideas to: • interpret and evaluate • make judgements and draw conclusions • develop and improve experimental procedures.	20
	Total	**100%**

Breakdown of Assessment Objectives

Paper	Assessment Objectives			Total for all Assessment Objectives
	AO1 %	AO2 %	AO3 %	
Paper 1: Biology 1 (F/H)	6.67	6.67	3.33	16.67 %
Paper 2: Biology 2 (F/H)	6.67	6.67	3.33	16.67 %
Paper 3: Chemistry 1 (F/H)	6.67	6.67	3.33	16.67 %
Paper 4: Chemistry 2 (F/H)	6.67	6.67	3.33	16.67 %
Paper 5: Physics 1 (F/H)	6.67	6.67	3.33	16.67 %
Paper 6: Physics 2 (F/H)	6.67	6.67	3.33	16.67 %
Total for GCSE	**40% ±3**	**40% ±3**	**20% ±3**	**100%**

Synoptic assessment

Synoptic assessment requires students to work across different parts of a qualification and to show their accumulated knowledge and understanding of a topic or subject area.

Synoptic assessment enables students to show their ability to combine their skills, knowledge and understanding with breadth and depth of the individual sciences.

Questions that naturally draw together different aspects of biology or chemistry or physics will assess synopticity.

Sample assessment materials

Sample papers and mark schemes can be found in the *Pearson Edexcel Level 1/Level 2 GCSE (9–1) in Combined Science* Sample *Assessment Materials* (SAMs) document.

4 Administration and general information

Entries

Details of how to enter students for the examinations for this qualification can be found in our *UK Information Manual*. A copy is made available to all examinations officers and is available on our website: qualifications.pearson.com

Forbidden combinations and discount code

Centres should be aware that students who enter for more than one GCSE, or other Level 2 qualifications with the same discount code, will have only the grade for their 'first entry' counted for the purpose of the School and College Performance Tables (please see *Appendix 10: Codes*). For further information about what constitutes 'first entry' and full details of how this policy is applied, please refer to the DfE website: www.education.gov.uk

Students should be advised that, if they take two GCSEs with the same discount code, schools and colleges to which they wish to progress are very likely to take the view that they have achieved only one of the two GCSEs. The same view may be taken if students take two GCSE or other Level 2 qualifications that have different discount codes but which have significant overlap of content. Students or their advisers who have any doubts about their subject combinations should check with the institution to which they wish to progress before embarking on their programmes.

Access arrangements, reasonable adjustments, special consideration and malpractice

Equality and fairness are central to our work. Our equality policy requires all students to have equal opportunity to access our qualifications and assessments, and our qualifications to be awarded in a way that is fair to every student.

We are committed to making sure that:

- students with a protected characteristic (as defined by the Equality Act 2010) are not, when they are undertaking one of our qualifications, disadvantaged in comparison to students who do not share that characteristic
- all students achieve the recognition they deserve for undertaking a qualification and that this achievement can be compared fairly to the achievement of their peers.

Language of assessment

Assessment of this qualification will be available in English. All student work must be in English.

Access arrangements

Access arrangements are agreed before an assessment. They allow students with special educational needs, disabilities or temporary injuries to:

- access the assessment
- show what they know and can do without changing the demands of the assessment.

The intention behind an access arrangement is to meet the particular needs of an individual student with a disability, without affecting the integrity of the assessment. Access arrangements are the principal way in which awarding bodies comply with the duty under the Equality Act 2010 to make 'reasonable adjustments'.

Access arrangements should always be processed at the start of the course. Students will then know what is available and have the access arrangement(s) in place for assessment.

Reasonable adjustments

The Equality Act 2010 requires an awarding organisation to make reasonable adjustments where a person with a disability would be at a substantial disadvantage in undertaking an assessment. The awarding organisation is required to take reasonable steps to overcome that disadvantage.

A reasonable adjustment for a particular person may be unique to that individual and therefore might not be in the list of available access arrangements.

Whether an adjustment will be considered reasonable will depend on a number of factors, which will include:

- the needs of the student with the disability
- the effectiveness of the adjustment
- the cost of the adjustment; and
- the likely impact of the adjustment on the student with the disability and other students.

An adjustment will not be approved if it involves unreasonable costs to the awarding organisation, timeframes or affects the security or integrity of the assessment. This is because the adjustment is not 'reasonable'.

Special consideration

Special consideration is a post-examination adjustment to a student's mark or grade to reflect temporary injury, illness or other indisposition at the time of the examination/ assessment, which has had, or is reasonably likely to have had, a material effect on a candidate's ability to take an assessment or demonstrate their level of attainment in an assessment.

Private candidates

Private candidates can complete this qualification only if they carry-out the mandatory core practicals with the centre in which they are sitting the exams, as long as the centre is willing to accept the candidate. These candidates need to fulfil the same requirements as all other candidates.

Further information

Please see our website for further information about how to apply for access arrangements and special consideration.

For further information about access arrangements, reasonable adjustments and special consideration, please refer to the JCQ website: www.jcq.org.uk.

Malpractice

Candidate malpractice

Candidate malpractice refers to any act by a candidate that compromises or seeks to compromise the process of assessment or which undermines the integrity of the qualifications or the validity of results/certificates.

Candidate malpractice in examinations **must** be reported to Pearson using a *JCQ M1 Form* (available at www.jcq.org.uk/exams-office/malpractice). The form can be emailed to pqsmalpractice@pearson.com or posted to Investigations Team, Pearson, 190 High Holborn, London, WC1V 7BH. Please provide as much information and supporting documentation as possible. Note that the final decision regarding appropriate sanctions lies with Pearson.

Failure to report malpractice constitutes staff or centre malpractice.

Staff/centre malpractice

Staff and centre malpractice includes both deliberate malpractice and maladministration of our qualifications. As with candidate malpractice, staff and centre malpractice is any act that compromises or seeks to compromise the process of assessment or which undermines the integrity of the qualifications or the validity of results/certificates.

All cases of suspected staff malpractice and maladministration **must** be reported immediately, before any investigation is undertaken by the centre, to Pearson on a *JCQ M2(a) Form* (available at www.jcq.org.uk/exams-office/malpractice). The form, supporting documentation and as much information as possible can be emailed to pqsmalpractice@pearson.com or posted to Investigations Team, Pearson, 190 High Holborn, London, WC1V 7BH. Note that the final decision regarding appropriate sanctions lies with Pearson.

Failure to report malpractice itself constitutes malpractice.

More-detailed guidance on malpractice can be found in the latest version of the document *JCQ General and Vocational Qualifications Suspected Malpractice in Examinations and Assessments,* available at www.jcq.org.uk/exams-office/malpractice.

Awarding and reporting

This qualification will be graded, awarded and certificated to comply with the requirements of Ofqual's General Conditions of Recognition.

This GCSE qualification will be graded and certificated on a 17-grade scale from 9–9 to 1–1 using the total subject mark where 9–9 is the highest grade. Individual papers are not graded. For foundation tier, grades 1–1 to 5–5 are available and for higher tier, grades 4–4 to 9–9 are available however if the mark achieved is a smaller number of marks below the 4–4 grade boundary, then a grade 4–3 may be awarded.

Students whose level of achievement is below the minimum judged by Pearson to be of sufficient standard to be recorded on a certificate will receive an unclassified U result.

The first certification opportunity for this qualification will be 2018.

Student recruitment and progression

Pearson follows the JCQ policy concerning recruitment to our qualifications in that:

- they must be available to anyone who is capable of reaching the required standard
- they must be free from barriers that restrict access and progression
- equal opportunities exist for all students.

Prior learning and other requirements

This qualification is based on the subject content, published by the DfE. The DfE designed the subject content to reflect or build on Key Stage 3. Consequently, students taking this qualification will benefit from previously studying Biology, Chemistry and Physics at Key Stage 3.

Progression

Students can progress from this qualification to:

- GCEs, for example in Biology, Chemistry and/or Physics
- Level 3 vocational qualifications in science, for example. BTEC Level 3 in Applied Science
- employment, for example in a science-based industry where an Apprenticeship may be available.

The content and skills for these qualifications are set by the DfE to be suitable to allow these progression routes.

Appendices

Appendix 1: Mathematical skills

This appendix is taken from the document *Combined Science GCSE subject content* published by the Department for Education (DfE) in June 2014.

The mathematical skills and use of mathematics statements listed will be assessed through the content of this qualification in the examinations. The minimum level of mathematics in the foundation tier examination papers will be equivalent to Key Stage 3 mathematics. The minimum level of mathematics in the higher tier examination papers will be equivalent to foundation tier GCSE in Mathematics.

Mathematical skills

Details of the mathematical skills in other science subjects are given for reference.

		Combined Science
1	**Arithmetic and numerical computation**	
a	Recognise and use expressions in decimal form	✓
b	Recognise and use expressions in standard form	✓
c	Use ratios, fractions and percentages	✓
d	Make estimates of the results of simple calculations	✓
2	**Handling data**	
a	Use an appropriate number of significant figures	✓
b	Find arithmetic means	✓
c	Construct and interpret frequency tables and diagrams, bar charts and histograms	✓
d	Understand the principles of sampling as applied to scientific data	✓
e	Understand simple probability	✓
f	Understand the terms mean, mode and median	✓
g	Use a scatter diagram to identify a correlation between two variables	✓
h	Make order of magnitude calculations	✓
3	**Algebra**	
a	Understand and use the symbols: $=, <, <<, >>, >, \propto, \sim$	✓
b	Change the subject of an equation	✓
c	Substitute numerical values into algebraic equations using appropriate units for physical quantities	✓
d	Solve simple algebraic equations	
4	**Graphs**	
a	Translate information between graphical and numeric form	✓
b	Understand that $y = mx + c$ represents a linear relationship	✓
c	Plot two variables from experimental or other data	✓
d	Determine the slope and intercept of a linear graph	✓
e	Draw and use the slope of a tangent to a curve as a measure of rate of change	✓
f	Understand the physical significance of area between a curve and the x-axis and measure it by counting squares as appropriate	✓

		Combined Science
5	**Geometry and trigonometry**	
a	Use angular measures in degrees	✓
b	Visualise and represent 2D and 3D forms, including two dimensional representations of 3D objects	✓
c	Calculate areas of triangles and rectangles, surface areas and volumes of cubes.	✓

Appendix 2: Taxonomy

The following table lists the command words used in the external assessments.

Command word	Definition
Add/Label	Requires the addition or labelling to a stimulus material given in the question, for example labelling a diagram or adding units to a table.
Assess	Give careful consideration to all the factors or events that apply and identify which are the most important or relevant. Make a judgement on the importance of something, and come to a conclusion where needed.
Calculate	Obtain a numerical answer, showing relevant working. If the answer has a unit, this must be included. This can include using an equation to calculate a numerical answer.
Comment on	Requires the synthesis of a number of variables from data/information to form a judgement.
Compare	Looking for the similarities **or** differences of two (or more) things. Should not require the drawing of a conclusion. Answer must relate to both (or all) things mentioned in the question.
Compare and contrast	Looking for the similarities **and** differences of two (or more) things. Should not require the drawing of a conclusion. Answer must relate to both (or all) things mentioned in the question. The answer must include at least one similarity and one difference.
Complete	Requires the completion of a table/diagram.
Deduce	Draw/reach conclusion(s) from the information provided.
Describe	To give an account of something. Statements in the response need to be developed as they are often linked but do not need to include a justification or reason.
Determine	The answer must have an element which is quantitative from the stimulus provided, or must show how the answer can be reached quantitatively. To gain maximum marks there must be a quantitative element to the answer.
Devise	Plan or invent a procedure from existing principles/ideas.
Discuss	Identify the issue/situation/problem/argument that is being assessed within the question. Explore all aspects of an issue/situation/problem/argument. Investigate the issue/situation etc. by reasoning or argument.
Draw	Produce a diagram either using a ruler or using freehand.
Estimate	Find an approximate value, number, or quantity from a diagram/given data or through a calculation.

Command word	Definition
Evaluate	Review information (e.g. data, methods) then bring it together to form a conclusion, drawing on evidence including strengths, weaknesses, alternative actions, relevant data or information. Come to a supported judgement of a subject's qualities and relation to its context.
Explain	An explanation requires a justification/exemplification of a point. The answer must contain some element of reasoning/justification, this can include mathematical explanations.
Give/State/Name	All of these command words are really synonyms. They generally all require recall of one or more pieces of information.
Give a reason/reasons	When a statement has been made and the requirement is only to give the reasons why.
Identify	Usually requires some key information to be selected from a given stimulus/resource.
Justify	Give evidence to support (either the statement given in the question or an earlier answer).
Measure	To determine the dimensions or angle from a diagram using an instrument such as a ruler or protractor.
Plot	Produce a graph by marking points accurately on a grid from data that is provided and then drawing a line of best fit through these points. A suitable scale and appropriately labelled axes must be included if these are not provided in the question.
Predict	Give an expected result.
Show that	Verify the statement given in the question.
Sketch	Produce a freehand drawing. For a graph this would need a line and labelled axis with important features indicated, the axis are not scaled.
State and explain	Make a point and link ideas to justify that point. An explanation requires a justification/exemplification of a point. The answer must contain some element of reasoning/justification, this can include mathematical explanations.
State what is meant by	When the meaning of a term is expected but there are different ways of how these can be described.
Write	When the questions ask for an equation.

Verbs preceding a command word	
Suggest a ...	Suggest an explanation or suggest a description.

Appendix 3: Periodic table

The Periodic Table of the Elements

Key

relative atomic mass
atomic symbol
name
atomic (proton) number

1	2											3	4	5	6	7	0
							1 **H** hydrogen 1										4 **He** helium 2
7 **Li** lithium 3	9 **Be** beryllium 4											11 **B** boron 5	12 **C** carbon 6	14 **N** nitrogen 7	16 **O** oxygen 8	19 **F** fluorine 9	20 **Ne** neon 10
23 **Na** sodium 11	24 **Mg** magnesium 12											27 **Al** aluminium 13	28 **Si** silicon 14	31 **P** phosphorus 15	32 **S** sulfur 16	35.5 **Cl** chlorine 17	40 **Ar** argon 18
39 **K** potassium 19	40 **Ca** calcium 20	45 **Sc** scandium 21	48 **Ti** titanium 22	51 **V** vanadium 23	52 **Cr** chromium 24	55 **Mn** manganese 25	56 **Fe** iron 26	59 **Co** cobalt 27	59 **Ni** nickel 28	63.5 **Cu** copper 29	65 **Zn** zinc 30	70 **Ga** gallium 31	73 **Ge** germanium 32	75 **As** arsenic 33	79 **Se** selenium 34	80 **Br** bromine 35	84 **Kr** krypton 36
85 **Rb** rubidium 37	88 **Sr** strontium 38	89 **Y** yttrium 39	91 **Zr** zirconium 40	93 **Nb** niobium 41	96 **Mo** molybdenum 42	[98] **Tc** technetium 43	101 **Ru** ruthenium 44	103 **Rh** rhodium 45	106 **Pd** palladium 46	108 **Ag** silver 47	112 **Cd** cadmium 48	115 **In** indium 49	119 **Sn** tin 50	122 **Sb** antimony 51	128 **Te** tellurium 52	127 **I** iodine 53	131 **Xe** xenon 54
133 **Cs** caesium 55	137 **Ba** barium 56	139 **La*** lanthanum 57	178 **Hf** hafnium 72	181 **Ta** tantalum 73	184 **W** tungsten 74	186 **Re** rhenium 75	190 **Os** osmium 76	192 **Ir** iridium 77	195 **Pt** platinum 78	197 **Au** gold 79	201 **Hg** mercury 80	204 **Tl** thallium 81	207 **Pb** lead 82	209 **Bi** bismuth 83	[209] **Po** polonium 84	[210] **At** astatine 85	[222] **Rn** radon 86
[223] **Fr** francium 87	[226] **Ra** radium 88	[227] **Ac*** actinium 89	[261] **Rf** rutherfordium 104	[262] **Db** dubnium 105	[266] **Sg** seaborgium 106	[264] **Bh** bohrium 107	[277] **Hs** hassium 108	[268] **Mt** meitnerium 109	[271] **Ds** darmstadtium 110	[272] **Rg** roentgenium 111	Elements with atomic numbers 112-116 have been reported but not fully authenticated						

***The lanthanoids (atomic numbers 58-71) and the actinoids (atomic numbers 90-103) have been omitted.**

The relative atomic masses of copper and chlorine have not been rounded to the nearest whole number.

Appendix 4: Equations in Combined Science

This appendix is taken from the document *Combined Science GCSE subject content* published by the Department for Education (DfE) in June 2014.

This identifies which equations students are required to recall and apply (list a) and which they are required to select from a list and apply (list b). List b also includes three additional equations to the DfE equations.

a Students should be able to recall and apply all the following equations

Students may be asked to recall, recall and apply, or only apply these equations in the exam papers. If students are required to only apply an equation from this section the equation will be given in the question.

Equations required for higher tier only are shown in bold text. Higher tier only equations will not be required in the foundation tier papers.

Specification reference	Equation
2.6b	distance travelled = average speed × time
2.8	acceleration = change in velocity ÷ time taken $a = \frac{(v - u)}{t}$
2.15	force = mass × acceleration $F = m \times a$
2.16	weight = mass × gravitational field strength $W = m \times g$
2.24	**momentum = mass × velocity** $\boldsymbol{p = m \times v}$
3.1 and 8.8	change in gravitational potential energy = mass × gravitational field strength × change in vertical height $\Delta GPE = m \times g \times \Delta h$
3.2 and 8.9	kinetic energy = $\frac{1}{2}$ × mass × (speed)^2 $KE = \frac{1}{2} \times m \times v^2$
3.11 and 8.15	efficiency = $\frac{\text{(useful energy transferred by the device)}}{\text{(total energy supplied to the device)}}$
4.6	wave speed = frequency × wavelength $v = f \times \lambda$
	wave speed = distance ÷ time $v = \frac{x}{t}$

Specification reference	Equation
8.6	work done = force × distance moved in the direction of the force $E = F \times d$
8.13	power = work done ÷ time taken $P = \frac{E}{t}$
10.6	energy transferred = charge moved × potential difference $E = Q \times V$
10.9	charge = current × time $Q = I \times t$
10.13	potential difference = current × resistance $V = I \times R$
10.29	power = energy transferred (joule, J) ÷ time taken $P = \frac{E}{t}$
10.31	electrical power = current × potential difference $P = I \times V$
	electrical power = (current)^2 × resistance $P = I^2 \times R$
14.2	Density = mass ÷ volume $\rho = \frac{m}{V}$
15.3	force exerted on a spring = spring constant × extension $F = k \times x$

b Students should be able to select and apply the following equations

Students may be asked to select and apply these equations in the exam papers. These equations will be given in a formulae sheet at the end of the exam papers.

Equations required for higher tier only are shown in bold text. Higher tier only equations will not be given in the formulae sheet for the foundation tier papers.

Specification reference	Equation
2.9	(final velocity)^2 – (initial velocity)^2 = 2 × acceleration × distance $v^2 - u^2 = 2 \times a \times x$
2.26	**force = change in momentum ÷ time** $\boldsymbol{F = \frac{(mv - mu)}{t}}$
10.27	energy transferred = current × potential difference × time $E = I \times V \times t$
12.13	**force on a conductor at right angles to a magnetic field carrying a current = magnetic flux density × current × length** $\boldsymbol{F = B \times I \times l}$
13.10	For transformers with 100% efficiency, potential difference across primary coil × current in primary coil = potential difference across secondary coil × current in secondary coil $V_P \times I_P = V_S \times I_s$
14.8	change in thermal energy = mass × specific heat capacity × change in temperature $\Delta Q = m \times c \times \Delta\theta$
14.9	thermal energy for a change of state = mass × specific latent heat $Q = m \times L$
15.4	energy transferred in stretching = 0.5 × spring constant × (extension)^2 $E = \frac{1}{2} \times k \times x^2$

Appendix 5: SI Units in Combined Science

This appendix is taken from the document *Combined Science GCSE subject content* published by the Department for Education (DfE) in June 2014.

The International System of Units (Système International d'Unités), which is abbreviated SI, is a coherent system of base units. The six which are relevant for the GCSE in Combined Science are listed below. Also listed are eight of the derived units (which have special names) selected from the SI list of derived units in the same source.

Base units

These units and their associated quantities are dimensionally independent.

metre

Unit symbol: **m**

kilogram

Unit symbol: **kg**

second

Unit symbol: **s**

ampere

Unit symbol: **A**

kelvin

Unit symbol: **K**

mole

Unit symbol: **mol**

Some derived units with special names

name	unit	abbreviation
Frequency	hertz	Hz
Force	newton	N
Energy	joule	J
Power	watt	W
Pressure	pascal	Pa
Electric charge	coulomb	C
Electric potential difference	volt	V
Electric resistance	ohm	Ω
Magnetic flux density	tesla	T

Appendix 6: Apparatus and techniques

The apparatus and techniques listed in the table below are taken from the document *Combined Science GCSE subject content* published by the Department for Education (DfE) in June 2014.

Use and coverage of the apparatus and techniques listed are mandatory. The 18 mandatory core practicals cover all aspects of the listed apparatus and techniques and are referenced in the table.

Safety is an overriding requirement for all practical work. Centres are responsible for ensuring that whenever their students complete practical work appropriate safety procedures are followed.

Scientific diagrams should be included, where appropriate, to show the set-up and to record the apparatus and procedures used in practical work.

BIOLOGY

	Apparatus and techniques	Core practical (specification reference)	
1	Use of appropriate apparatus to make and record a range of measurements accurately, including length, area, mass, time, temperature, volume of liquids and gases, and pH	1.6	*Investigate biological specimens using microscopes, including magnification calculations and labelled scientific drawings from observations*
		1.10	*Investigate the effect of pH on enzyme activity*
		1.16	*Investigate osmosis in potatoes*
		6.5	*Investigate the effect of light intensity on the rate of photosynthesis*
		8.11	*Investigate the rate of respiration in living organisms*
		9.5	*Investigate the relationship between organisms and their environment using field-work techniques, including quadrats and belt transects*
2	Safe use of appropriate heating devices and techniques, including use of a Bunsen burner and a water bath or electric heater	1.10	*Investigate the effect of pH on enzyme activity*
		6.5	*Investigate the effect of light intensity on the rate of photosynthesis*
		8.11	*Investigate the rate of respiration in living organisms*
3	Use of appropriate apparatus and techniques for the observation and measurement of biological changes and/or processes	1.6	*Investigate biological specimens using microscopes, including magnification calculations and labelled scientific drawings from observations*
		1.10	*Investigate the effect of pH on enzyme activity*
		1.16	*Investigate osmosis in potatoes*
		6.5	*Investigate the effect of light intensity on the rate of photosynthesis*
		8.11	*Investigate the rate of respiration in living organisms*

	Apparatus and techniques	Core practical (specification reference)	
4	Safe and ethical use of living organisms (plants or animals) to measure physiological functions and responses to the environment	6.5	*Investigate the effect of light intensity on the rate of photosynthesis*
		8.11	*Investigate the rate of respiration in living organisms*
		9.5	*Investigate the relationship between organisms and their environment using field-work techniques, including quadrats and belt transects*
5	Measurement of rates of reaction by a variety of methods, including production of gas, uptake of water and colour change of indicator	1.10	*Investigate the effect of pH on enzyme activity*
		1.16	*Investigate osmosis in potatoes*
		6.5	*Investigate the effect of light intensity on the rate of photosynthesis*
		8.11	*Investigate the rate of respiration in living organisms*
6	Application of appropriate sampling techniques to investigate the distribution and abundance of organisms in an ecosystem via direct use in the field	9.5	*Investigate the relationship between organisms and their environment using field-work techniques, including quadrats and belt transects*
7	Use of appropriate apparatus, techniques and magnification, including microscopes, to make observations of biological specimens and produce labelled scientific drawings	1.6	*Investigate biological specimens using microscopes, including magnification calculations and labelled scientific drawings from observations*
		9.5	*Investigate the relationship between organisms and their environment using field-work techniques, including quadrats and belt transects*

CHEMISTRY

	Apparatus and techniques	Core practical (specification reference)
1	Use of appropriate apparatus to make and record a range of measurements accurately, including mass, time, temperature, and volume of liquids and gases	2.11 *Investigate the composition of inks using simple distillation and paper chromatography* 3.6 *Investigate the change in pH on adding powdered calcium hydroxide or calcium oxide to a fixed volume of dilute hydrochloric acid* 3.17 *Investigate the preparation of pure, dry hydrated copper sulfate crystals starting from copper oxide including the use of a water bath* 3.31 *Investigate the electrolysis of copper sulfate solution with inert electrodes and copper electrodes* *7.1* *Investigate the effects of changing the conditions of a reaction on the rates of chemical reactions by:* *a measuring the production of a gas (in the reaction between hydrochloric acid and marble chips)* *b observing a colour change (in the reaction between sodium thiosulfate and hydrochloric acid)*
2	Safe use of appropriate heating devices and techniques including use of a Bunsen burner and a water bath or electric heater	2.11 *Investigate the composition of inks using simple distillation and paper chromatography* 3.17 *Investigate the preparation of pure, dry hydrated copper sulfate crystals starting from copper oxide including the use of a water bath* *7.1* *Investigate the effects of changing the conditions of a reaction on the rates of chemical reactions by:* *a measuring the production of a gas (in the reaction between hydrochloric acid and marble chips)* *b observing a colour change (in the reaction between sodium thiosulfate and hydrochloric acid)*

	Apparatus and techniques	Core practical (specification reference)	
3	Use of appropriate apparatus and techniques for conducting and monitoring chemical reactions, including appropriate reagents and/or techniques for the measurement of pH in different situations	3.6	*Investigate the change in pH on adding powdered calcium hydroxide or calcium oxide to a fixed volume of dilute hydrochloric acid*
		3.31	*Investigate the electrolysis of copper sulfate solution with inert electrodes and copper electrodes*
		7.1	*Investigate the effects of changing the conditions of a reaction on the rates of chemical reactions by:* *a* *measuring the production of a gas (in the reaction between hydrochloric acid and marble chips)* *b* *observing a colour change (in the reaction between sodium thiosulfate and hydrochloric acid)*
4	Safe use of a range of equipment to purify and/or separate chemical mixtures including evaporation, filtration, crystallisation, chromatography and distillation	2.11	*Investigate the composition of inks using simple distillation and paper chromatography*
		3.17	*Investigate the preparation of pure, dry hydrated copper sulfate crystals starting from copper oxide including the use of a water bath*
5	Making and recording of appropriate observations during chemical reactions including changes in temperature and the measurement of rates of reaction by a variety of methods such as production of gas and colour change	3.6	*Investigate the change in pH on adding powdered calcium hydroxide or calcium oxide to a fixed volume of dilute hydrochloric acid*
		7.1	*Investigate the effects of changing the conditions of a reaction on the rates of chemical reactions by:* *a* *measuring the production of a gas (in the reaction between hydrochloric acid and marble chips)* *b* *observing a colour change (in the reaction between sodium thiosulfate and hydrochloric acid)*

	Apparatus and techniques		Core practical (specification reference)
6	Safe use and careful handling of gases, liquids and solids, including careful mixing of reagents under controlled conditions, using appropriate apparatus to explore chemical changes and/or products	2.11	*Investigate the composition of inks using simple distillation and paper chromatography*
		3.6	*Investigate the change in pH on adding powdered calcium hydroxide or calcium oxide to a fixed volume of dilute hydrochloric acid*
		3.17	*Investigate the preparation of pure, dry hydrated copper sulfate crystals starting from copper oxide including the use of a water bath*
		3.31	*Investigate the electrolysis of copper sulfate solution with inert electrodes and copper electrodes*
		7.1	*Investigate the effects of changing the conditions of a reaction on the rates of chemical reactions by:* *a measuring the production of a gas (in the reaction between hydrochloric acid and marble chips)* *b observing a colour change (in the reaction between sodium thiosulfate and hydrochloric acid)*
7	Use of appropriate apparatus and techniques to draw, set up and use electrochemical cells for separation and production of elements and compounds	3.31	*Investigate the electrolysis of copper sulfate solution with inert electrodes and copper electrodes*

PHYSICS

	Apparatus and techniques	Core practical (specification reference)	
1	Use of appropriate apparatus to make and record a range of measurements accurately, including length, area, mass, time, volume and temperature. Use of such measurements to determine densities of solid and liquid objects.	2.19	*Investigate the relationship between force, mass and acceleration by varying the masses added to trolleys*
		4.17	*Investigate the suitability of equipment to measure the speed, frequency and wavelength of a wave in a solid and a fluid*
		14.3	*Investigate the densities of solid and liquids*
		14.11	*Investigate the properties of water by determining the specific heat capacity of water and obtaining a temperature-time graph for melting ice*
2	Use of appropriate apparatus to measure and observe the effects of forces including the extension of springs	2.19	*Investigate the relationship between force, mass and acceleration by varying the masses added to trolleys*
		15.6	*Investigate the extension and work done when applying forces to a spring*
3	Use of appropriate apparatus and techniques for measuring motion, including determination of speed and rate of change of speed (acceleration/deceleration)	2.19	*Investigate the relationship between force, mass and acceleration by varying the masses added to trolleys*
4	Making observations of waves in fluids and solids to identify the suitability of apparatus to measure speed/frequency/ wavelength. Making observations of the effects of the interaction of electromagnetic waves with matter.	4.17	*Investigate the suitability of equipment to measure the speed, frequency and wavelength of a wave in a solid and a fluid*
		5.9	*Investigate refraction in rectangular glass blocks in terms of the interaction of electromagnetic waves with matter*
5	Safe use of appropriate apparatus in a range of contexts to measure energy changes/transfers and associated values such as work done	14.11	*Investigate the properties of water by determining the specific heat capacity of water and obtaining a temperature-time graph for melting ice*
		15.6	*Investigate the extension and work done when applying forces to a spring*

	Apparatus and techniques	Core practical (specification reference)
6	Use of appropriate apparatus to measure current, potential difference (voltage) and resistance, and to explore the characteristics of a variety of circuit elements	10.17 *Construct electrical circuits to:* a *investigate the relationship between potential difference, current and resistance for a resistor and a filament lamp* b *test series and parallel circuits using resistors and filament lamps*
7	Use of circuit diagrams to construct and check series and parallel circuits including a variety of common circuit elements	10.17 *Construct electrical circuits to:* a *investigate the relationship between potential difference, current and resistance for a resistor and a filament lamp* b *test series and parallel circuits using resistors and filament lamps*

These core practicals may be reviewed and amended if changes are required to the apparatus and techniques listed by the Department for Education. Pearson may also review and amend the core practicals if necessary. Centres will be told about any changes as soon as possible.

You must follow the instructions in the table below for each core practical.

BIOLOGY

	Core practical	Description
1.6	*Investigate biological specimens using microscopes including magnification calculations and labelled scientific drawings from observations*	This practical allows students to develop their skills in using a light microscope, preparing slides, and producing labelled scientific drawings. Students need to be familiar with the set-up and use of a light microscope, as well as to be able to identify structures that they see. Magnification calculations will also be required.
1.10	*Investigate the effect of pH on enzyme activity*	For this core practical students will investigate the effect of pH, however other variables can also be investigated to enhance practical work in this area. This method uses amylase (in solutions of different pH) to break down starch. The reaction can be monitored by using iodine to test the presence of starch in the solution with a continuous sampling method. To maintain the temperature of the solution, a Bunsen burner and water beaker must be used.

Core practical		Description
1.16	*Investigate osmosis in potatoes*	A known mass of potato must be added to sucrose solution, left for some time, and the final mass recorded to obtain the percentage change in mass. This investigation looks at the exchange of water between the potato and solution and allows the concentration of sucrose in the potato to be determined. The practical provides an opportunity for the appreciation of the need to control variables.
6.5	*Investigate the effect of light intensity on the rate of photosynthesis*	Algal balls (or similar) must be set up and placed at varying distances from a light source to investigate the effect of light intensity on the rate of photosynthesis. The rate must be measured and compared to the distance away from the light source.
8.11	*Investigate the rate of respiration in living organisms*	Use of a simple respirometer to measure the effect of temperature on the oxygen consumption of some small organisms. A simple respirometer can be made using a tube with soda lime, cotton wool and organisms with a capillary tube to coloured liquid. Students can then track the progress of the liquid up the capillary tube over a set time. This experiment must be carried out using a water bath set at different temperatures. Safety and ethical considerations must also be covered.
9.5	*Investigate the relationship between organisms and their environment using field-work techniques, including quadrats and belt transects*	This investigation involves the use of a belt transect along a gradient (e.g. shaded area to an area with no shade). It involves students thinking about how to sample their chosen area, including the identification and observation of plants/organisms.

CHEMISTRY

Core practical		Description
2.11	*Investigate the composition of inks using simple distillation and paper chromatography*	This core practical is in two parts; a simple chromatography practical to obtain a chromatogram of dyes in ink and using simple distillation apparatus to separate pure water from ink. It needs to cover usage of a Bunsen burner, methods used in chromatography and distillation and safety of handling liquids.
3.6	*Investigate the change in pH on adding powdered calcium hydroxide or calcium oxide to a fixed volume of dilute hydrochloric acid*	This practical focuses on recording the pH at intervals when calcium hydroxide or calcium oxide reacts with dilute hydrochloric acid. An initial mass of the solid must be added to a fixed volume of the acid, and the pH recorded each time more of the solid is added to the acid. The pH can be recorded using a pH meter, or universal indicator paper with a glass rod used to take a pH measurement at each interval.
3.17	*Investigate the preparation of pure, dry hydrated copper sulfate crystals starting from copper oxide including the use of a water bath*	Excess copper oxide must be added to warm dilute sulfuric acid (warmed using a water bath), which will react to produce a blue solution of the salt copper(II) sulfate. The solution then needs to be filtered using filter paper and evaporated using an evaporating basin and Bunsen burner, followed by final drying using a watch glass to allow all the water to evaporate.
3.31	*Investigate the electrolysis of copper sulfate solution with inert electrodes and copper electrodes*	This involves setting up an electrolysis to investigate the effect of changing the current on the mass of the copper electrodes used in the electrolysis of copper sulfate solution. The second part of this investigation covers the products formed during the electrolysis of copper sulfate solution using inert (graphite) electrodes. Quantitative analysis when using copper electrodes will be expected.

	Core practical	Description
7.1	*Investigate the effects of changing the conditions of a reaction on the rates of chemical reactions by:* *a measuring the production of a gas (in the reaction between hydrochloric acid and marble chips)* *b observing a colour change (in the reaction between sodium thiosulfate and hydrochloric acid)*	This investigation is in two parts. Both parts require the reaction to be observed with respect to time to obtain the rate. In the first part, marble chips must be added to hydrochloric acid, and the volume of gas collected and measured over time. This will lead to graphical analysis to calculate rate, as well as an appreciation for how the rate may change with varying concentration of acid/temperature/surface area of marble chips. The second part involves sodium thiosulfate reacting with dilute hydrochloric acid to produce a precipitate using the idea of a 'disappearing cross' to observe the change in the appearance of the reaction mixture as a precipitate of sulfur is formed. This must be carried out at different temperatures by warming the thiosulfate solution. A graph must be drawn to show the time taken for the reaction to take place at different temperatures.

PHYSICS

	Core practical	Description
2.19	*Investigate the relationship between force, mass and acceleration by varying the masses added to trolleys*	Different masses must be used to investigate the effect of varying masses on the acceleration of a trolley down a ramp. Appropriate methods must be used to measure the force and time taken for the trolley to travel down the ramp, and data analysis must include calculating the acceleration.
4.17	*Investigate the suitability of equipment to measure the speed, frequency and wavelength of a wave in a solid and a fluid*	This investigation involves looking at the characteristics of waves and using the equation: $v = f \times \lambda$ It is expected that students will have looked at waves in a liquid using a ripple tank, and waves in a solid using a metal rod and a method of measuring the frequency. Suitability of apparatus to take these measurements must also be considered.
5.9	*Investigate refraction in rectangular glass blocks in terms of the interaction of electromagnetic waves with matter*	A light source with grating must be used to produce a beam of light, which must then be used to investigate the effect of refraction using a glass block. An appreciation of the interaction of the light ray with the glass block and the effect of changing medium on the light ray (moving towards and away from the normal) must be included.

Core practical		Description
10.17	*Construct electrical circuits to:* *a investigate the relationship between potential difference, current and resistance for a resistor and a filament lamp* *b test series and parallel circuits using resistors and filament lamps*	This investigation involves constructing a circuit to investigate potential difference, current and resistance for a resistor and a filament lamp. The behaviour of parallel and series circuits must also be included, and this must be done using filament lamps. A series circuit should be set up initially with a resistor, ammeter and voltmeter. The current must be recorded at different voltages. This must then be repeated using a filament lamp instead of a resistor. To investigate series and parallel circuits, a parallel circuit must be set up with ammeters, voltmeters, and filament lamps. Readings from this circuit must then be compared with series circuits used initially. Analysis must include use of the equation: $V = I \times R$
14.3	*Investigate the densities of solid and liquids*	The density of a solid object must be determined by measuring the mass and volume of the object, and then using the equation: $\rho = \frac{m}{v}$ The volume must be determined by putting the object into water, and measuring the volume of water that has been displaced. The density of a liquid can be calculated by weighing the liquid using a balance, and determining the volume. The equation: $\rho = \frac{m}{v}$ must then be used to calculate the density.
14.11	*Investigate the properties of water by determining the specific heat capacity of water and obtaining a temperature-time graph for melting ice*	The temperature of crushed ice must be recorded using a thermometer. This must then be melted using a Bunsen burner and beaker of water as a water bath. The temperature must be monitored as the ice melts. To determine specific heat capacity of water, the temperature of water using a thermometer must be monitored while heating it using a heat supply connected to a joulemeter. This must then be used to calculate the specific heat capacity.
15.6	*Investigate the extension and work done when applying forces to a spring*	The stretching of a spring must be investigated by measuring the length of a spring with no weights, followed by adding varying masses and measuring the new length. This must include calculating the work done and an appreciation of the forces involved.

Appendix 7: Practical Science Statement

Pearson Edexcel Level 1/Level 2 GCSE (9–1) in Combined Science	**1SC0**
Centre name:	Centre number:

All candidates must carry out the 18 mandatory core practicals throughout the course of this qualification.

Details of practical work

Biology

Core practicals:

1.6	*Investigate biological specimens using microscopes, including magnification calculations and labelled scientific drawings from observations*
1.10	*Investigate the effect of pH on enzyme activity*
1.16	*Investigate osmosis in potatoes*
5.5	*Investigate the effect of light intensity on the rate of photosynthesis*
8.11	*Investigate the rate of respiration in living organisms*
9.5	*Investigate the relationship between organisms and their environment using field-work techniques, including quadrats and belt transects*

Chemistry

Core practicals:

2.11	*Investigate the composition of inks using simple distillation and paper chromatography*
3.6	*Investigate the change in pH on adding powdered calcium hydroxide or calcium oxide to a fixed volume of dilute hydrochloric acid*
3.17	*Investigate the preparation of pure, dry hydrated copper sulfate crystals starting from copper oxide including the use of a water bath*
3.31	*Investigate the electrolysis of copper sulfate solution with inert electrodes and copper electrodes*
7.1	*Core Practical: Investigate the effects of changing the conditions of a reaction on the rates of chemical reactions by:* *a measuring the production of a gas (in the reaction between hydrochloric acid and marble chips)* *b observing a colour change (in the reaction between sodium thiosulfate and hydrochloric acid)*

Physics

Core practicals:

2.19	*Investigate the relationship between force, mass and acceleration by varying the masses added to trolleys*
4.17	*Investigate the suitability of equipment to measure the speed, frequency and wavelength of a wave in a solid and a fluid*
5.9	*Investigate refraction in rectangular glass blocks in terms of the interaction of electromagnetic waves with matter*
10.17	*Construct electrical circuits to:*
	a investigate the relationship between potential difference, current and resistance for a resistor and a filament lamp
	b test series and parallel circuits using resistors and filament lamps
14.3	*Investigate the densities of solid and liquids*
14.11	*Investigate the properties of water by determining the specific heat capacity of water and obtaining a temperature-time graph for melting ice*
15.6	*Investigate the extension and work done when applying forces to a spring*

Head teacher declaration

I declare that each candidate has completed the practical activities set out above in accordance with Pearson Edexcel Level 1/Level 2 GCSE in Combined Science (9–1) practical science work requirements.

Each candidate has made a contemporaneous record of:

i the work that they have undertaken during these practical activities, and

ii the knowledge, skills and understanding they have derived from those practical activities.

Head teacher name:			
Head teacher signature:		**Date:**	

Appendix 8: The context for the development of this qualification

All our qualifications are designed to meet our World Class Qualification Principles[1] and our ambition to put the student at the heart of everything we do.

We have developed and designed this qualification by:

- reviewing other curricula and qualifications to ensure that it is comparable with those taken in high-performing jurisdictions overseas
- consulting with key stakeholders on content and assessment, including learned bodies, subject associations, higher education academics and teachers to ensure this qualification is suitable for a UK context
- reviewing the legacy qualification and building on its positive attributes.

This qualification has also been developed to meet criteria stipulated by Ofqual in their documents *GCSE (9 to 1) Qualification Level Conditions and Requirements* and *GCSE Subject Level Conditions and Requirements for Combined Science*, published in April 2014.

---

[1] Pearson's World Class Qualification Principles ensure that our qualifications are:

- **demanding**, through internationally benchmarked standards, encouraging deep learning and measuring higher-order skills
- **rigorous**, through setting and maintaining standards over time, developing reliable and valid assessment tasks and processes, and generating confidence in end users of the knowledge, skills and competencies of certified students
- **inclusive**, through conceptualising learning as continuous, recognising that students develop at different rates and have different learning needs, and focusing on progression
- **empowering**, through promoting the development of transferable skills, see *Appendix 9*.

From Pearson's Expert Panel for World Class Qualifications

" The reform of the qualifications system in England is a profoundly important change to the education system. Teachers need to know that the new qualifications will assist them in helping their learners make progress in their lives.

When these changes were first proposed we were approached by Pearson to join an 'Expert Panel' that would advise them on the development of the new qualifications.

We were chosen, either because of our expertise in the UK education system, or because of our experience in reforming qualifications in other systems around the world as diverse as Singapore, Hong Kong, Australia and a number of countries across Europe.

We have guided Pearson through what we judge to be a rigorous qualification development process that has included:

- Extensive international comparability of subject content against the highest-performing jurisdictions in the world
- Benchmarking assessments against UK and overseas providers to ensure that they are at the right level of demand
- Establishing External Subject Advisory Groups, drawing on independent subject-specific expertise to challenge and validate our qualifications
- Subjecting the final qualifications to scrutiny against the DfE content and Ofqual accreditation criteria in advance of submission.

Importantly, we have worked to ensure that the content and learning is future oriented. The design has been guided by what is called an 'Efficacy Framework', meaning learner outcomes have been at the heart of this development throughout.

We understand that ultimately it is excellent teaching that is the key factor to a learner's success in education. As a result of our work as a panel we are confident that we have supported the development of qualifications that are outstanding for their coherence, thoroughness and attention to detail and can be regarded as representing world-class best practice. "

Sir Michael Barber (Chair)

Chief Education Advisor, Pearson plc

Bahram Bekhradnia

President, Higher Education Policy Institute

Dame Sally Coates

Principal, Burlington Danes Academy

Professor Robin Coningham

Pro-Vice Chancellor, University of Durham

Dr Peter Hill

Former Chief Executive ACARA

Professor Sing Kong Lee

Director, National Institute of Education, Singapore

Professor Jonathan Osborne

Stanford University

Professor Dr Ursula Renold

Federal Institute of Technology, Switzerland

Professor Bob Schwartz

Harvard Graduate School of Education

Appendix 9: Transferable skills

The need for transferable skills

In recent years, higher education institutions and employers have consistently flagged the need for students to develop a range of transferable skills to enable them to respond with confidence to the demands of undergraduate study and the world of work.

The Organisation for Economic Co-operation and Development (OECD) defines skills, or competencies, as 'the bundle of knowledge, attributes and capacities that can be learned and that enable individuals to successfully and consistently perform an activity or task and can be built upon and extended through learning.' [1]

To support the design of our qualifications, the Pearson Research Team selected and evaluated seven global 21st-century skills frameworks. Following on from this process, we identified the National Research Council's (NRC) framework as the most evidence-based and robust skills framework. We adapted the framework slightly to include the Program for International Student Assessment (PISA) ICT Literacy and Collaborative Problem Solving (CPS) Skills.

The adapted National Research Council's framework of skills involves: [2]

Cognitive skills

- **Non-routine problem solving** – expert thinking, metacognition, creativity.
- **Systems thinking** – decision making and reasoning.
- **Critical thinking** – definitions of critical thinking are broad and usually involve general cognitive skills such as analysing, synthesising and reasoning skills.
- **ICT literacy** – access, manage, integrate, evaluate, construct and communicate. [3]

Interpersonal skills

- **Communication** – active listening, oral communication, written communication, assertive communication and non-verbal communication.
- **Relationship-building skills** – teamwork, trust, intercultural sensitivity, service orientation, self-presentation, social influence, conflict resolution and negotiation.
- **Collaborative problem solving** – establishing and maintaining shared understanding, taking appropriate action, establishing and maintaining team organisation.

Intrapersonal skills

- **Adaptability** – ability and willingness to cope with the uncertain, handling work stress, adapting to different personalities, communication styles and cultures, and physical adaptability to various indoor and outdoor work environments.
- **Self-management and self-development** – ability to work remotely in virtual teams, work autonomously, be self-motivating and self-monitoring, willing and able to acquire new information and skills related to work.

Transferable skills enable young people to face the demands of further and higher education, as well as the demands of the workplace, and are important in the teaching and learning of this qualification. We will provide teaching and learning materials, developed with stakeholders, to support our qualifications.

---

[1] OECD (2012), Better Skills, Better Jobs, Better Lives (2012): http://skills.oecd.org/documents/OECDSkillsStrategyFINALENG.pdf

[2] Koenig, J. A. (2011) *Assessing 21st Century Skills: Summary of a Workshop*, National Research Council

[3] PISA (2011) The PISA Framework for Assessment of ICT Literacy, PISA

Appendix 10: Codes

Type of code	Use of code	Code
Discount codes	Every qualification is assigned to a discount code indicating the subject area to which it belongs. This code may change. See our website (qualifications.pearson.com) for details of any changes.	RA1B
National Qualifications Framework (NQF) codes	Each qualification title is allocated an Ofqual National Qualifications Framework (NQF) code. The NQF code is known as a Qualification Number (QN). This is the code that features in the DfE Section 96 and on the LARA as being eligible for 16–18 and 19+ funding, and is to be used for all qualification funding purposes. The QN will appear on students' final certification documentation.	The QN for this qualification is: 601/8612/4
Subject codes	The subject code is used by centres to enter students for a qualification. Centres will need to use the entry codes only when claiming students' qualifications.	GCSE in Combined Science – 1SC0
Paper codes	These codes are provided for reference purposes. Students need to be entered for individual papers at the same tier.	Paper 1: 1SC0/1BF, 1SC0/1BH Paper 2: 1SC0/2BF, 1SC0/2BH Paper 3: 1SC0/1CF, 1SC0/1CH Paper 4: 1SC0/2CF, 1SC0/2CH Paper 5: 1SC0/1PF, 1SC0/1PH Paper 6: 1SC0/2PF, 1SC0/2PH

Sb210316Z:\LT\PD\GCSE 2016\9780997865370_GCSE2016_L12_COMBSCI\9780997865370_GCSE2016_L12_COMBSCI.DOC.1–118/7

Edexcel, BTEC and LCCI qualifications

Edexcel, BTEC and LCCI qualifications are awarded by Pearson, the UK's largest awarding body offering academic and vocational qualifications that are globally recognised and benchmarked. For further information, please visit our qualification websites at www.edexcel.com, www.btec.co.uk or www.lcci.org.uk. Alternatively, you can get in touch with us using the details on our contact us page at qualifications.pearson.com/contactus

About Pearson

Pearson is the world's leading learning company, with 40,000 employees in more than 70 countries working to help people of all ages to make measurable progress in their lives through learning. We put the learner at the centre of everything we do, because wherever learning flourishes, so do people. Find out more about how we can help you and your learners at qualifications.pearson.com

Original origami artwork: Mark Bolitho
Origami photography: Pearson Education Ltd/Naki Kouyioumtzis

ISBN 978 0 997 86537 0